Ruining

Me

Nicole Reed

ISBN-13: 978-1481955300
ISBN-10: 1481955306

Find out more Nicole and any upcoming books online at:
www.nicolreed.wordpress.com
or
www.facebook.com/RuiningMe

Chapter One

Two years ago, I learned the hard way that every moment of our lives defines everything we are and everything we will be. These moments either bind us deeply to reality or sever the ties that bind us to it. In those precious seconds, we must decide which path we will choose: the path of life or the path of death.

My path has been chosen, and my time on this earth is limited. I know this with every single breath I take, with every sunrise and sunset I see. I have total control of it. It will be my choice, my time, and my decision, but today is not that day. Today, I look around me at the same sight I have seen every morning for the past three years. The same brick building that I stood staring up at my freshman year. The sign on the front reads Jackson Heights High School.

Looking up at the massive two-story building, I can honestly say that I will not miss it. At all. It's my first day of senior year, and by all accounts, it should be the best one yet. After all, it's the one everyone has looked forward to since the first day of kindergarten when they stepped into the hallowed walls of a school building. I, however, am not the girl I once was. I see my old best friends, Molly and Reed, sitting on the entrance steps laughing. Turning back to the parking lot, I spot JT Higgins, my ex-boyfriend, smiling and kissing the one that replaced me, Stacie Courtman, while leaning against his shiny red Ford truck. I guess we have all moved forward.

My focus drifts back to Molly. Her red hair shines brightly in the morning sun almost like it is on fire. She glares at me and leans down to whisper something to Reed. He raises his dark eyes, and they both stare. Looking down at my feet, the pain consumes me. I know I'm not the only one remembering how close we once were. Our parents had been friends in college, and we all grew up on the same street. "Thick as thieves," my dad used to say. There is not a single childhood memory that doesn't involve them. My heart begins to ache, and my eyes glaze with tears I thought I could no longer shed.

Taking a deep breath, I compose myself. It's a hot muggy Georgia morning, and if I stand here knee-deep in memories any longer, I may melt. Even in a barely there yellow t-shirt, blue jean mini just long enough to avoid a trip to the principal's office, and a pair of yellow low-top Converse, I'm sweating or, as my southern grandmother would say, "glistening." Thankfully, I pulled my long dark hair up into a ponytail this morning, and my choice to wear nothing but lip gloss means no ridiculous colors are sliding off my face.

Walking toward the steps, I hear a deep voice from behind me.

"Hey James. Wait up."

Yes, I have a boy's name. My mother named me after her grandfather who raised her, but all my friends call me Jay. I turn to see Caleb Myers smiling back at me. Cal and I go way back to kindergarten where we bonded over food. I used to feed him my lunch all through elementary school, and somehow in his mind, this equated to best friend status. Now, he is a two-hundred plus pound rock solid teddy bear, and a starting offensive lineman for the Jackson Heights Bulldogs. He is also the one person that I can still talk to. When everyone ditched me as the result of my relentless cold shoulder and bitchy ways, he kept coming back for more. After a while, he wore on me, and I decided that I would just have to get used to the big guy. Cal throws his massive arm around my shoulders and gives me a sloppy wet kiss on the cheek.

"Geez, Cal. Happy to see me?" I can't help smiling.

"Yeah girl, it's been a long hot ass summer, and we are finally seniors. We're gonna rule the school and all that shit. Now, tell me how much you missed me."

I chuckle because, honestly, I have missed him. I chose to ignore his hundred million text messages and calls this past summer and kept to myself just like the previous year. My motto was no lake, no parties, and no people. My smile fades as I glance up at him. He looks serious all of a sudden. Cal moves his hand to gently lift my chin and looks into my eyes.

"Jay, I've been thinking, and I need to get this out. This is our last year in high school. You can change things. It's not too late." I grab his hand in an effort push it away from my face, but he holds tighter. "Don't do this. Don't keep pushing everyone away," he says as his eyes plead with mine.

The painful sincerity in his eyes takes my breath away. Somehow, it's like he knows my secrets and my intentions. Shaking my head, I force his hand from my face.

"You don't know what you are talking about, Cal. Just leave it alone," I say to him.

"It doesn't have to be this way, Jay. Everyone misses you, and we want the old you back."

"We? As in your best friend JT? I don't think so, Cal. He was "making out" with his new girlfriend in the parking lot. It really looked like he was missing me," I respond sarcastically. Pain laced my voice.

"What? You want him begging at your heels after you screwed everyone else but him?"

My eyes almost bulge out of my head. Cal looks shocked those words came out of his mouth, and before he can say anything else, I hurriedly walk the other direction. I hastily climb the steps and squeeze through the front doors passing Molly and Reed and pushing back the tears, just as I've pushed them all away.

I don't know what it is about the first day of school. There is so much anticipation in the air you can taste it, and even I am not immune. Keeping my eyes down, I walk directly to my first period class. I'm one of the first students to arrive in homeroom. My teacher, Mrs. Davis, glances up when I walk in, and she greets me with a smile.

"Well, Miss James Stevenson. How was your summer?"

"Fine," I answer and smile back.

Walking to the back of the classroom, I grab a desk and drop my book bag beside it. Pretty soon, the class starts to fill up, and the gossip of the summer begins. I take notice when Cal walks in the room, but thankfully, there are no seats in my general vicinity. Bowing my head, I grab my notebook and prepare for class. I've learned that keeping to myself is easier if I just avoid looking at anyone. Mrs. Davis finally starts talking, and before I know it, the bell rings and first period is over. I'm able to slip out without having to talk with Cal.

I head straight to my second period class, Biology. As I enter the room, I glance up and see Rhye Clark sitting in the back. Rhye is the average high school bad boy with his dark shaggy hair, intensely dark chocolate eye, and a long lanky frame. His black faded skinny jeans are painted on him, and his band's name, The Mavs, stands out against his black t-shirt. His rock star image is completed with piercings in his eyebrow and lip and tattoos running the length of both arms. I'm pretty sure that his glazed look has something more to do with what he smoked this morning and not that his band probably played somewhere downtown until late last night.

His eyes brighten when he notices me, and he shoots me a sexy grin. Trying to get my attention, he nods his head toward the seat next to him. I pointedly roll my eyes and take a seat on the other side of the room. There was a time that I thought taking control of my life meant controlling who I slept with. My first conquest was Rhye. He flirted with me for years, and the moment JT and I were over, he quickly moved in. Rhye and his lifestyle became like my drug of choice, and he loved corrupting me almost a little too much.

I can feel his eyes burning into me the entire class. In the couple of months I spent as his "friend with benefits," I learned the advantages of dating the bad boy. Unfortunately, that also included learning that even high school band lead singers have groupies. I can be easy, but I don't share, and Rhye learned that lesson a little too late. When the bell finally rings, I gather my books and stuff them in my bag.

"How was your summer, Jay?"

His voice is low and sexy. Damn those dark eyes. I stand up and look at him.

"Great. Thanks for asking."

I walk out of the class room and can hear him following right behind me.

"Did you not get the little messages I sent to you?"

I stop suddenly and whirl around to face him. Does he have to be so freaking hot? Stepping towards him and looking directly into his eyes, I place my pointed finger into his chest.

"Yes, I did, and I need you to be less stalkerish. Now, grow the fuck up and move on Rhye! You cheated on me. Remember?"

He winces, and pain fills his dark eyes. For a moment, I think he may regret what happened. "Damn, Jay. It's almost been a year. I messed up. Just let that shit die. I want you to come watch us play."

Rolling my eyes, I turn to walk away. I feel his hand circle my wrist, and he gently tugs me back around and pulls me closer.

"I wouldn't mind if you want to stay the night afterwards either. I'm sure we could think of something to do."

"Dream on rock star. My groupie days are over."

This time, when I turn to walk away, he lets go. I hear him chuckle, and I groan. He is just too sexy for my own good. It's getting harder and harder to turn him away, but I think that's his plan. He is slowly wearing me down.

Third period is a study period, and I pass the hour hiding out in the library. When the bell finally rings for lunch, I am surprised that so much of the day has passed. Although the Georgia heat is enough to keep anyone inside, the sunshine lures me to a seat outside. Most everyone respects that I like to keep to myself. Only a few dare to attempt a conversation with me, and usually, my one word answers are enough to deter them. I hear the whispers of "stuck-up" and "what a bitch". I should be used to it by now, but it still stings. I catch myself smiling when someone smiles at me. After all, it's hard to go from the school sweetheart, to well, whatever I am now. I take a seat, and delve into my book.

Looking up, I notice JT staring at me. His eyes are the perfect shade of a deep midnight blue. Sighing, I remember a time when I could look into those eyes for hours and see my future for miles and miles. Now, I'm not so sure what I would see.

JT had the perfect girlfriend, and in a moment, she was gone. He tried for weeks to talk to me, and he even camped outside my bedroom window. I thought my dad was going to kill him when he pitched his Boy Scout tent on the lawn. I finally told him there was someone else, and that was the end. If I had known it was that easy, I would have lied earlier. Well, really, it wasn't a lie.

Glancing back at my book, I see a pair of black Nike shoes step next to me. I look up and have to shield my eyes from the sun to see JT glaring down. It's hard to look into those eyes that I used to dream about, so I look away, unable to bear it. He must have stepped in front of the sun's rays because I can't feel them on my face anymore. I sit in his shade.

"What can I do for you, JT?"

My voice sounds breathy, and my eyes shift back to him. He still does this to me. My body begins to slightly shake from nerves, and I can't help but to still want him. In that second, I remember every moment. My mind races to our first kiss in the seventh grade. It was beautifully innocent.

"How was your summer, Jay?" His voice sounds so angry. It startles me for a second, but he continues to speak. "Kip says he saw you downtown at O'Malley's a couple of times. Guess you were giving that fake ID a workout, huh?"

Kip is JT's older brother who attends the local college. I still talk to Kip when I see him, but we never discuss JT. He slowly lowers his body down to look me in the eyes. "Are you too good to hang out with us kiddies?" I don't think he realizes that his words are weapons, and each one cuts me deep enough to bleed.

"Wow, JT! I didn't know you missed me so much. I figured you were too busy screwing Stacie all summer," I say sarcastically. I couldn't help myself. I am hemorrhaging from the inside out. The people I do associate with like to gossip, and I had already heard this tidbit of information through the grapevine. As soon as I say it, I wish I hadn't. I still care. JT's cheeks redden, and he leans in closer.

"Anytime you want that to be you, just let me know." He then stands up and walks away. There was a time that I prayed for that to happen and to be that girl, but that time has passed.

Before I know it, school is over, and I am walking out to my car thinking about my last couple of classes. I ended up in another class with Cal, and fortunately for me, he just shook his head and let me be. Fifth period was Art, and both Reed and Molly were in it. The teacher, Miss Kell, talked about our goals for the year, so no one had a chance to talk. Last period was P.E., and just my luck, I ended up in class with JT. We didn't speak.

With my thoughts on everything that happened today, I almost miss the piece of paper caught underneath my yellow Ford Mustang's windshield wiper. I know what it is before I even read it. Damn. I was really hoping this would be the year he quit sending them. I yank it off and wad it into my hand. I ignored his little attempts to get my attention last year, and I prayed this year he would give me a freaking break. Apparently, that's not going to happen. My mind knows I should just throw it away, but I open it anyway.

I can't stop thinking about you.

He's smart. The notes are typed. There is no way to trace their origin even if I wanted to. Ripping it up and tossing it to the ground, I get in my car and drive away.

Not feeling like going home, I head downtown. No one is home anyway. Both my parents own and operate a small airfield outside of town. My mother and father are both licensed private pilots for the rich and famous. Georgia is the new Hollywood "It" spot for making movies, and my parents are cashing in. Carting around celebrities keeps them away from home, but it doesn't bother me. In fact, it's probably for the best. Lately, any time we spend together ends with a fight.

Traffic is light this time of day, and I decide to drive to my favorite bar. Living on the outskirts of a big college town has its advantages. Within twenty minutes, I can be at some of the best bars around. O'Malley's is where most of the young college crowd hangs out, and it's my favorite. It's eighteen to enter and twenty-one to drink. My fake ID says I'm both. O'Malley's looks like an Irish pub during the day, but at night, it comes alive with live music, packed pool tables, and rocking dance floor.

As I walk in, I hear a Mazzy Star song playing in the background. Not many people are here at four o'clock in the afternoon. I've made friends with the daytime bartender, Jill. She is about six feet tall and looks as though she would be right at home on a volleyball court with her California girl looks. Jill is in her late twenties and finishing up her Master's degree in Education. She smiles when she sees me climb onto the barstool.

"Hey Jay, how was the dreaded first day of school?"

"Just kill me now. Yes, it was that awful." I cross my arms on the bar and lay my head on top of them. I groan and ask, "Can I get a Sprite?" Jill laughs and fixes my drink.

"Sure, baby girl. So, I haven't seen you around these past couple of weeks. Have you met the new weekend bartender?"

I shake my head while sipping my Sprite, and she continues.

"Oh my God, he is so hot. Seriously fuckable. He's about six foot two with dark buzzed hair. He's got amazingly cut arms, and don't even get me started on his stomach. One night he pulled his t-shirt up, and he's got a serious six pack. Oh, and his butt? You could bounce a quarter off of it."

I spit out my drink all over the bar in response to her description of his butt.

Laughing, Jill grabs a rag and starts to wipe my mess, "I didn't know that people could actually have eyes that green, and he's got the coolest tats on both of his arms and neck. The man is pulling in some serious tips from the college girls. If I wasn't in a serious relationship right now, I'd be right there with them," she gushes.

Jill is constantly trying to hook me up, and she scouts all the beaus from the buttholes. She knows I'm only looking for one night stands, and she is my safety net. I've learned that most bartenders know who and what is going down in their bars. Jill starts talking to me again, pulling me away from my thoughts.

"I've worked with him a couple of times, and he seems super nice. He just moved to town to work for his family. His brother owns a construction company, and he has a daytime job with him, but with the economy being what it is, he supplements his income with bartending. He's twenty-three, never been married, and no kids. Seems he is from somewhere in the Midwest originally, and get this, he's single," she says letting the last word linger on a happy tune. I start to say how he just doesn't sound like my type, considering his age, when the door behind the bar swings open.

In walks the description of perfection Jill just finished telling me about. He smiles at her and just says, "Hi." He glances around and finally notices me. We stare at each other for a split second. He grins, nods his head toward me, and turns away to ask Jill something about his work schedule.

Now, I know most guys consider me good looking. I admit that I have never lacked attention in school, but, to be honest, I have never understood what guys see in me. I don't have extraordinarily beautiful hair or a flawlessly curvy body like Molly's, and my eyes lend to a dull gray opposed to vibrant blue. I'm not saying I'm not cute. I just don't consider myself gorgeous. However, in this moment, I wanted to be noticed. Lust almost doubles me over in my seat, but there is something more. I swear, something else passed through his eyes a moment ago.

My eyes drink him in. He is a tall glass of water with his closely shaved dark hair and shiny emerald eyes. He has a strong nose and nice full lips. His tight black t-shirt hugs his huge biceps, and black tribal swirls travel down his left arm. His right arm is covered in a full tattoo sleeve. He has some black writing on the side of his neck that I am unable to read. Blue jeans mold around his behind. Jill totally got that part right. I can see why he is making good tips now.

Finally, I allow my eyes to travel back up to his face, and, oh my goodness, he is smiling at me. He has not one, but two adorable dimples adorning his cheeks. He turns away from Jill and towards me.

"Like what you see, sweetheart?" His voice sounds hoarse and super sexy.

It takes a moment for my brain to catch up, and when it does, for some reason, I am pissed by his remark. What a conceited jackass and a total turn off for me. I should have known with his looks that he couldn't possibly have a good personality.

"Not anymore, sweetie," I reply snidely back. I take a swig of my drink and look back at Jill. He bursts out laughing, takes a step toward me, and leans over the bar.

"Okay, that's fair. Can I say that I like what I see?"

His voice pulls at something deep down inside me. I know his type, and all they want is for girls to pet their oversized egos and other things below the belt. I definitely wouldn't give him that satisfaction. Narrowing my eyes at him and with an evil smile, I say, "That depends. What is it that you see?"

"Now, that could be the trickiest question a woman has ever asked me. So, I guess I will stick with the truth and say that I see a dark haired beauty with eyes the color of a stormy sea sitting in front of me." My heart momentarily melts until he continues to speak, "or

I could be honest with us both and tell you how a minute ago I saw those same stormy eyes devouring me from head to toe."

I couldn't control the next words that flew out of my mouth. "What a conceited ass! I like eye candy as much as the next girl, but you soon learn the truth about candy."

He laughs louder this time. "What? That it melts in your mouth and not in your hand?"

Damn it! That sexy smile and voice are getting to me. "You wish," I reply with a laugh. I cannot believe he just said that, and I simply shake my head.

"I have to fucking ask then. Just what is this truth about candy?"

I move in close to him as to whisper my answer, and he leans in. Our lips are only inches away from each other, and his gaze breaks from eyes and drifts down to my mouth. I intentionally lick my lips and answer him. "Wouldn't you like to know?"

His eyes return to mine, and we stare at each other. He finally blinks and grins.

"That is so lame. I mean, really, that's all you got?"

I shrug my shoulders and glance back to Jill. Her eyes have been volleying back and forth between us during the conversation. She finally laughs and nudges his shoulder.

"I guess I'll do the introductions. Kane, this is my friend Jay. Jay, this is the new bartender Kane. Both of you need to play nice while I go back and get the schedule worked out."

I look down at my Sprite and realize it's gone.

"Can I get you a refill?"

"No thanks, I'm good," I answer. I try looking everywhere but at him. I can feel his eyes on me, and it's driving me crazy.

"Would you like to go out sometime?"

"I don't think so."

"What, are you afraid of going cross-eyed from staring at me all night?"

I shoot him my mean look, and he laughs again.

"I'm just kidding. Really, I would like to take you out though.

Don't make me beg." He tilts his head and waits for my answer.

"I don't think I'm your type."

"Ok, this is going to be good. Go ahead and tell me what my type is." He's still grinning at me.

"I would bet that your last two girlfriends were blonde and big-breasted." His eyebrows go up in question.

"You got something against blonde and big-breasted? And good guess, but I'm not confirming or denying it." He leans back so that he can look me up and down this time. "However, I'm finding out right now that I like them dark-haired and sassy."

My heart rate suddenly spikes, and I wonder if he can hear the loud thumping. If he was any other guy with these looks, I would be trying to take him home for the night whether he's a conceited ass or not. But something in me says Kane is different. One night wouldn't be enough for either of us. Where did that thought come from? I need to get out of here.

"Um, can you please tell Jill I had to run," I say as I stand and grab my bag. I take a five dollar bill out of my purse and lay it on the bar. Geez, my freaking hand is shaking. Glancing one more time into his eyes, I notice he looks confused. I gather not too many girls brush him off.

"Hey, don't leave. I'm not actually working tonight and plan on just hanging out and playing some pool. Why don't you stay a little while longer? You can tell me all about my type and I can find out the truth about candy."

His question really throws me off. I look at him, and confusion lingers on his face.

"Sorry, I've got places to be. Nice meeting you," I answer and turn to flee. My escape would have been okay, if I had seen the stool standing in front of me. Unfortunately, I trip over the bottom rung and the seat catches me mid-stomach. My breath whooshes out, and I fall to my knees. I think he actually jumped over the bar to intercept me, but I'm not sure.

"Are you okay?" He asks leaning down and placing his arm on

my back.

His touch makes my breathing very shallow, and I glance to his face. My eyes lower to his plump bottom lip just inches from mine. Staring at them as they move, I realize he is asking if I am okay. Holy shit, am I okay? I shake my head "no" at first, but then I remember to answer him.

"Yes." It is a whisper, but I know he hears me. His eyes move towards my mouth, and I can't help pulling in my bottom lip and sucking on it. I hear him groan, and the sound startles me. Jumping up, I break away from his touch. His eyes look dazed and confused. In a second attempt to escape, I turn and walk away while thanking God he didn't follow.

My thoughts are scattered the whole way home. I have never felt this pull with anyone else, not even with JT. Just the thought of him makes my cheeks flush. Dear Jesus, he is as hot as Hades. He has the longest black eye lashes to set off those gorgeous eyes. Post JT, I really don't do relationships. Well, I mean other than Rhye, but that was totally different.

Most people at school think that I have become a slut. The truth is I'm far from it. I'm very selective, which is why I enlist Jill to help. Plus, it's not every night and not even close to every month. It's just when I have that need, and to clarify, it is not a need to have sex. It's more of a need to have control of who I give my body to. I subscribe to the whole "love them and leave them" philosophy. That's more my style, and I really do not like these feelings I am having about Kane. It already feels like more, and I've only known him for five seconds. I have to stop thinking about the stupid conceited jackass.

My phone is buzzing as I pull my car into my driveway signaling an incoming text message. Noticing it is from Jill, I read it.

Jill – He wants your #. BAD. Do you want me to give it to him? He's asking 20 million ?'s. Not sure what you want me to say.

I decide to ignore her because my mind is spinning. As I open my door, I hear the roar of an engine. Looking behind me, a black 4x4 truck pulls in. Cal practically jumps out before his truck even comes to a complete stop.

"Jay, I'm really sorry about today. I left football practice early because I was worried you were mad at me. I shouldn't have said what I did." Cal looks upset, and he keeps rambling as he walks towards me. "I know whatever shit made you like you is none of my business. I've just been really worried about you, and I can't explain it, but I wanted to come and talk to you tonight."

He actually looks sick. What is it about this guy that I can't stay mad at him?

"Listen Cal, we're good." I put my hands up because he looks like he is going to hug me. "But for the future, stay out of my business, and we'll be just fine." I look toward my dark empty house and realize that I didn't want to be alone right now. "Want to come in and have dinner?"

Cal's face lights up. "Have I ever turned you down when you offered me food? I would even eat that nasty cafeteria spaghetti in fourth grade because I didn't want you to get in trouble for not eating your lunch."

"I never knew that. I thought you either really loved that stuff or you were starving."

"No way, Jay, that shit was nasty. I would only eat it for you," he says and grins at me. I can't help but smile back as I realize that Cal has always been there for me.

chapter Two

The sun is starting to set as Cal and I walk into the house and straight through to the kitchen. My parents and I live in an upper middle class non-gated golf community. Our house is a two-story monstrosity that overlooks a golf hole and a large pond. Our kitchen could be straight out of a high end restaurant despite the fact we never cook. We have a lady who comes in twice a week to clean, and she usually cooks and freezes dinners for the week too. I sit my iPhone in the dock and turn on some music. While I pull out a pan of lasagna from the freezer unthaw in the microwave, the acoustic version of "Scream" by Chris Cornell, fills the quiet.

Standing behind me, Cal asks, "What can I do to help you with dinner, Jay?"

"Thanks Cal, but I've got it. Just have a seat at the bar." He plops down on one of barstools.

"So, where did you go after school?" Cal asks.

Ignoring him at first, I grab the lettuce and salad dressing from the fridge and lay them on the counter. Finally looking at him, I want to tell him that it is none of his business, but I am tired of being snappy to him. I've reached my limit for the day.

"Well, I've gotten to be friends with one of the bartenders at O'Malley's, so I went to talk with her."

Cal looks at me and says, "I heard that you were hanging out there a lot."

"Yeah, you and everyone else," my voice snaps at him. He seems hurt by my attitude. Saved by the beeps of the microwave, I take the lasagna out. I figure we would eat at the counter, so I pass Cal a plate and silverware.

"Soda okay?" I ask and grab him a can from the refrigerator.

"Actually, do you have any milk?"

"Sure," I reply and pour him a glass. We both eat in silence for a while. Even though I had wanted his company, I keep thinking about Kane.

"Penny for your thoughts," Cal said.

I'm not sure why, but all of a sudden, I begin talking about meeting Kane.

"So, was it love at first sight?" Cal's question throws me off.

"I don't know that I believe in that; however, I do believe in lust at first sight. I would definitely say there was some serious lusting going on," I say laughingly as I hear him cough. Cal must have choked on his food when I said that.

After a couple of minutes of coughing, he finally looks at me and says, "Not sure what to say to that, Jay." His cheeks blush as he takes a large sip of milk.

When I look up at him, I notice he has a milk mustache. I catch his eye between bites of food and wink saying, "Milk does a body good, huh?" His expression is priceless, and his face turns beet red. Geez, does he think I'm hitting on him? I laugh.

"Cal, you have a milk mustache."

He grabs his napkin and wipes his mouth while he laughs for a second. "For a moment there, I thought I was going to have to fight you off, girl. I didn't know if all this lust talk was getting to you." We smile at each other and continue eating. "Not that I would fight you off, you know." He wags his eyebrows at me, and we both laugh.

When we finish eating, I begin putting the food away.

"So, we're good, huh?" He stands and grabs our plates to put them in the dishwasher. Leaning against the counter, he crosses his arms and looks at me.

The overhead light shines on his surfer blond hair, and his face still has that baby look to it. I move to stand across from him as he clears his throat.

"I just want to say one more thing before I leave. You know, a lot of people miss you. Miss seeing that smiling face every morning, and not just the students. I know that several of the football coaches have even mentioned that they miss seeing you on the sidelines. During football season, even when we lost a game, you kept everyone's spirits up. You were there all the way up until our sophomore year. I never played one football game, even little league, that you weren't on the sidelines. Hell, even Coach Branch last year told us all to keep an eye on you. You just don't know...," Cal stops talking as I glare at him.

"What do you mean, Coach Branch told you to keep an eye on me?"

Cal looks confused by my question and continues, "He just asked the linemen to keep an eye on you last year. He said he noticed that you were having a hard time. You know how he cares about his students. Coach B and his wife had twins this summer, and he still took his own time to help us seniors get ready for the college scouts. He just really cares about what happens to all of us. They're guys on the football and baseball team that wouldn't even be going to college if it weren't for him helping them to get scholarships."

"Well, that is nice, but I don't need anyone looking out for me. Please make sure you tell all of the guys that I said that," I reply heavy with sarcasm. "Look Cal, it's getting late. I'm okay, really. I just don't need everyone all in my business." I smile and walk out of the kitchen to the front door, letting him silently know that this conversation was over.

Cal stops as he walks out through the front door and turns back around. "I'm always going to be here. Just know that okay? Thanks for dinner." He leans in and kisses my cheek before turning to walk away.

Closing the door as he leaves, I hear my phone vibrate. The buzzing was present all through dinner, but the day's series of events led me to ignore it. Turning the house alarm on, I walk upstairs. It is still pretty early, but I shower and fall asleep on my bed.

Opening my eyes, I glance around me. I am sitting in a room with four walls and no doors. All the walls were white and scratched to hell. White metal chairs line them and in all the chairs sit women of different ages, sizes, and colors. We all have on white hospital gowns, and our protruding bellies are grotesquely round, almost as if we had swallowed basketballs. The women all have empty black sockets where their eyes should be. Their lips are sewn shut with what looks like twine.

I hear a metal chair screech as someone sits down next to me. Knowing who I would see as I turn my head, I look at him. He is always so beautiful. Wavy hair as black as ink and the darkest eyes I have ever seen are laced with thick black lashes. He has high cheekbones and a square jaw. His body is trim, and he is dressed to the nines in, what I would guess is, an Armani suit. He's always barefoot, but even his feet are beautiful.

Smiling at me, he props his arm across the back of my seat, and his voice, when he speaks, is deep. "**Yea, they sacrificed their sons and their daughters unto devils, and shed innocent blood, even the blood of their sons and of their daughters, whom they sacrificed unto the idols of Canaan: and the land was polluted with blood. Thus were they defiled with their own works, and went a whoring with their own inventions.** *Pretty much sums it up, doesn't it, babe?" I stare back at him.*

Satan wasn't ugly. I had always been taught in church that he was the most beautiful angel, and even in my dreams, I realize this. The women start humming what sounds like a lullaby. Their distended stomachs moving with what looks like little hands, stretching out from the inside of their bellies. I feel his hand start to touch my stomach, and I grab it to push him away. He looks down at me and says, "Why James, I just want to feel our baby. See how he reaches for his Daddy?" I look down, and a little hand is pushing up from the inside of my stomach. I start to scream.

I wake with my scream vibrating off the wall. Damn, I hadn't had a nightmare in months. Damn, damn, damn. I lay back down. Normally, I don't dream again once I wake up. My thoughts didn't slow down for quite a while, but finally, I drift back to sleep.

The next morning, I stand drinking coffee in the kitchen when I remember all the text messages from the day before. I grab my phone to check them. All of them are from Jill, except the last one. It was from a number I didn't recognize, which I assume after reading the text message, belongs to Kane.

Jill – Can you please let me know what to do with HIM????
He wants your number.

Jill – What did you do to this guy? He will not leave me alone.

Jill – CALL ME

569-423-1277 – You can't run. Meet me at O'Malley's tom night at 9. Were you going to tell me that candy rots your teeth?? Is that what they say about candy??? ☺

I actually laugh at his text message. God, he's such a jackass, but he's a hot one. I program his number in my phone, reach for my keys on the counter, and hurry to school. Running late, I speed into the parking lot and jog inside.

The warning bell rings as I walk into the school. Not looking where I'm going, I run right into Rhye. He grabs my waist and pulls me towards him.

"Slow down, Jay. You don't want to get hurt." One dark eye winks at me as his jet black hair falls across his forehead.

"Really, Rhye? Get your hands off of me." I turn out of his grasp and walk away as I hear his parting reply.

"I like it when you play hard to get. It only makes me want you more."

I don't even glance back, choosing to ignore him.

The morning passes, and lunch period arrives. I need to run out to my car and grab my phone. As I walk out of the school doors, Coach Branch is walking in.

He has been the offensive line coach and head baseball coach since I was a freshman. Back then, he was just out of college, but it didn't take long before our school thought of him as a hero. He was the reason our offensive linemen rated at the top in the State, and we had won the State Championship in baseball for our division every year since he started. Needless to say, our little community thought he walked on water. Plus, all the girls loved him and considered him a cutie. He had thick brown wavy hair and brown eyes that stood out with a baby face. He is pretty short and stocky for a guy. His southern accent was thick at times. I heard his wife was his college girlfriend, and I had met her at several different school functions. She was gorgeous and seemed nice.

"Well, Miss Stevenson, where are you headed?" he asks.

I am stunned for a moment. He starts to smile and say something else when Miss Kell, my Art teacher, walks up behind him. Coach Branch looks at her and shakes his head, as if he was nodding her to walk on by. Miss Kell stops and looks between us then finally, at me.

"James, are you okay? You look like you don't feel well."

My eyes shift between them both.

"Um, I left something in my car and was going to get it, but actually I don't need it."

I turn swiftly around and almost sprint down the hallway. Running into the girl's bathroom, I barely make it to the toilet before I start dry heaving. Ten minutes later, I wash my mouth out with some water and head for my next class.

During Art class, Miss Kell asks me again if I am okay. Nodding my head, I assure her that I am. This is the class that I have with Molly and Reed. We all used to spend a lot of our time drawing when we were little. In fact, I'm pretty sure that Reed got into some fancy art school up north, and I knew Molly was headed to the University of Georgia.

We receive our assignment, and I start to paint a stormy beach scene. After a while, I notice Molly and Reed laughing and joking with each other. Molly is smiling at something he had painted. At that moment, she looks up and sees me staring at her. Frowning, she suddenly looks down at her painting. Reed grabs her hand and whispers something in her ear, and then he looks up at me. Raising my brush, I start to paint again. I had already let them go, but it never got any easier. Every day was a reminder of what I had lost. Finally, the bell rings signaling the end of class.

I rush into the locker room to change into my shorts and a t-shirt for P.E. We are working out today with Coach Sanders, the head football coach. The school has a huge weight lifting and workout room. I intend to do some light weight lifting for toning. I like to keep my body in shape and make the most of my strength. In the corner, the guys were seeing who could bench press the most, and the girls were inflating the guys' already oversized egos by standing around them and cheering them on.

I had just lifted a dumbbell behind my head to work my triceps, when I feel someone pulling down on the weight behind me. Looking forward into the mirror, I notice JT standing there.

"Did you just see me bench 325?"

JT has on athletic shorts and a ripped t-shirt. He has grown so much these past two years. When did this boy become a man? I don't turn around and keep staring in the mirror attempting to finish my set.

"I figured you had enough fans," I huff out. He narrows his eyes. I did not push him away for the last couple of years to go back there again. "Go away, JT, before your girlfriend gets mad." I just want him to walk away, but I haven't been that lucky lately.

"So, I heard that you cooked for Cal last night. Are you screwing my best friend now?"

I bring the weight back over my head and to my chest. Turning to glare at him, I ask, "What the hell, JT? Is that what Cal said?" I know Cal would never say that, but I had to ask.

"No, Cal didn't say anything. I just heard that he told a couple of the guys that he had dinner at your house last night." He lowers his voice almost to a whisper and says, "I just can't stand the thought, okay. Not Cal, not anybody. I need to talk with you. I think we can work things out. Jay, I just need...."

I jump up and drop the weight on his toe before he can finish his sentence.

"Fuck!" He yells, and everyone turns to stare. I take off for the locker room and hurry to put my clothes on. I finish getting dressed right as the final bell rings. I sprint out to the parking lot before anyone else could happen to run into me. Of course, another message is on my car, so I yank it out from under the wiper and throw it to the ground. My eyes look up, and I watch JT hauling ass across the asphalt. I hurry to get into my car and leave with only one last look in the rear view mirror. JT is standing in the middle of the parking lot. My life sucks.

At home, I shower first and finally check my phone.

Rhye – call me...band playing tonight at Vortex. Want u there ...

I delete it immediately and read the other ones.

Jill – Call me. What happened with Kane?

MOM – Dad and I are flying back from Cali tomorrow. Let me know if you need anything. Love ya.

Cal – Everything okay with you and JT???

I decide to call Jill back right then. She picks up on the first ring, and before I could even say anything, she starts talking.

"I am so sorry, Jay. He grabbed my phone and stole your number. Damn, baby girl, what did you do to him? I swear both of your eyes couldn't take in each other fast enough, and there was so much electricity that my hair stood on end. Then all of a sudden, you're gone and he's asking me a million and one questions, but I swear I didn't tell him anything. I kept saying that I would talk with you first, but when you didn't text me back immediately, he made me start calling. When I still didn't hear from you, he just took my phone."

"It's okay, Jill. He sent me a text about meeting him there tonight. Look, you know how much I hang out at the bar, and I think a one night stand with him could make things difficult. You know, with him being an employee and all?"

"No offense Jay, but the vibes I had from you both didn't feel like one night stand vibes. I'm not saying that you shouldn't totally throw caution to the wind and jump into bed with him, but I'm not sure that is all it is. Jay, I get your situation. You are young and, believe me, if I knew in my own youth what I know now I would have been a player. You don't want anything serious, but I'm not sure what I saw or felt yesterday will go away quickly for either of you."

I groan into the phone, "I know Jill, that's why I am not going to meet him tonight. Please don't say anything though. I'm hoping he'll get the hint. I don't think he will take no for an answer."

Jill laughs, and I'm pretty sure she murmurs, "Good luck with that." I tell her I will see her sometime next week, and we hang up.

Around seven o'clock, I start thinking about him. I was trying to kid myself into thinking that he wouldn't really care whether or not I showed up. He would probably have a bimbo in the wings waiting. Not ever being the type to wait around on a guy myself, I decide to get dressed and head downtown. Slipping on a pair of tight jeans and a black, sexy, off-the-shoulder shirt, I start to feel better. The shiny black heels that I bought last week complete my look. I brush out my hair and spray on some perfume.

The drive takes a little longer because of traffic. When I left my house, I wasn't exactly sure where I was going. I didn't want to go to O'Malley's because that is where Kane would be, and Rhye would be at Vortex. There are several more bars downtown, but those two are my favorite. I decide on Vortex, not wanting to think too hard on why.

I find a parking space and flip my ID to the bouncer outside the doors. He marks my hand with an "over 21" stamp. As I walk in, I see a good number of people already hanging out. Vortex is a large room in a converted warehouse with the stage on one side and the bar on the other. In between, there are tables and booths and a small dance floor in front of the stage. Until the band goes on, rock music plays overhead.

It is eight o'clock, and Rhye's band wouldn't be on until ten. For now, I knew that they would be in the corner hanging out in their booth. The guys in the band are older than Rhye and me, but I had gotten to know them pretty well when we "dated."

Walking directly to the bar, I do not look to see if Rhye is around. The bartender is a girl that I do not know. She looks at my hand stamp to verify my age.

"What can I get you to drink?"

"Vodka and cranberry, please."

She fixes my drink, and I hand over money for the cocktail along with a great tip. My mouth puckers as I take a sip of the stout drink.

"Thanks," I say and turn around. A couple of cute guys are checking me out, but all I can think about are vibrant green eyes and that tattoo on the side of Kane's neck. I should have read it, because now it's driving me crazy just thinking about it. The stool next to me is pushed back as someone steps up beside me at the bar.

"Well, well, if it isn't Jay."

I turn to that voice that still makes my body come alive. Rhye is smiling at me. His eyes are glassy, but I can tell he is still lucid. He looks over my figure, and his gaze lingers on my breasts a little longer than the rest of me.

"I'm just here for the music, Rhye. Not to be your fuck buddy." I take a sip of my drink and glance at the people starting to move on the dance floor. Flyleaf's, "Something I Can Never Have," starts to play. He grabs my drink and sits it back on the bar so he can reach for my hand.

"Come dance with me, Jay?" His question catches me off guard. Rhye never liked to dance unless he was totally out of it.

24

"I didn't think you danced?" I am curious as to what his answer will be, but he doesn't say anything.

He pulls me to the dance floor and straight into his arms, moving his body fluidly against mine. I'm stunned for a second. It is obvious that he has learned a few moves since we were last together. My hips rock against his, and I follow his lead, letting the music take over. He sings the song gently in my ear, and I close my eyes, praying my knees will not give out.

Towards the end of the song, warm lips touch my shoulder. The first song turns into the second, and it is a slower rock ballad. I am already lost dancing with him. This is what he always offered me, a chance to forget everything. Both of his hands move down my body and grip my hips.

"Tell me what it will take, Jay?" His voice whispers in my ear. "I want you." His lips rub back and forth against my neck.

I raise my eyes to his face, and his dark eyes bore into mine. Shaking my head, I stop moving and think to myself, "This is a mistake." Rhye must have guessed my intention to pull away because, in that moment, he captures my mouth with his. His lips are hard against mine as he nips at my upper lip when I don't open up. I jerk away from him.

"Damn it, Rhye," I shout at him and break away from his grip. Heading straight to the bar, I order a beer. When I turn back around, he is gone. I glance in the direction of his booth and see that he is sitting with the band, staring at me. He knows if he pushes me, I will leave, and for some reason, he wants me to stay to hear him sing.

At about fifteen after nine, my phone vibrates with a text message.

Kane – Where R U

Ignoring it, I slip my phone back into my jeans pocket and take a sip of my beer.

The next hour passes pretty quickly. Rhye doesn't attempt to talk to me again. A couple of the guys in the band walk over to say, "Hi," but that's it. The bar starts to fill up as it gets closer to the band's performance.

When Rhye walks out on the stage, everyone goes crazy. He has so much charisma that I wouldn't be surprised to see him make it big one day. He waves his arms downward to try and silence the crowd.

"What's up, everybody? Glad you all could join us at the V tonight. You want to hear us play some music?" The crowd screams for them. The first two songs must have been new. I do not recognize the first one, and right before he starts to sing the second, he hushes the crowd.

"Okay, this next one I wrote about a girl that I can't get out of my mind. I know you guys know what I'm talking about." I swear he says it directly to me as he looks across the crowd.

The guitarist begins playing a slow melody. Rhye closes his eyes and begins singing. His words stun me.

"Her eyes haunt me when I close mine
I can't imagine what secrets they hold
But if she'll give me just one moment
I will remove all that pain from her soul.

I was careless when I held her
If I could do it all just once more
I won't make the same mistake
And let her walk out the door.

So it's your voice that I hear
And it's all in my head
And it's your pain that I feel
But you're not here instead

I want to take it all away
Take it all away
Take it all away"

I don't stay to hear the rest. I just walk out of the bar knowing he was talking about me. How dare he write that song? I don't want a song about me. My mind races as I walk to my car and drive away. He cheated on me, the rat bastard. How could he?

By the time I arrive home, it is almost eleven o'clock. I am too wound up to sleep, so I decide to watch a chick flick. Something with Channing Tatum so I could forget all the real-life eye candy I have to deal with. Throwing on my Juicy sweat pants and tank top, I pull my hair up. Nights like this, when I need someone to talk to, I really miss Molly and Reed. I almost pick up the phone and call Molly, but I'm pretty sure she would just hang up on me.

Several minutes into the movie, I decide to run down to the kitchen to get a drink when I hear the sound of a motorcycle. Mr. Mounts, our next door neighbor, must be going through one of his Harley phases again. A couple minutes later, the doorbell rings. It's almost eleven thirty, and I'm not sure who would be coming by this late.

Our front door is all beveled glass, except for the center circular window which is clear. As I walk to open it, I notice Kane looking at me. He is wearing a black leather jacket, and he looks pretty pissed. I turn the alarm off and open the door. Leaning against the frame not allowing him to enter, I cross my arms. He doesn't say anything at first as he stares at my face, and then he slowly sweeps his gaze downward. My body lights up like a circuit board. God, I ache just looking at him, and looking lower, it seems like I'm not the only one affected.

"It's late, and I'd love to know how you found out where I live."

"I asked some of the regulars at the bar if they knew you," he said in that sexy scratchy voice of his. "Some guy named Kip knew exactly where you lived. Do you want to tell me how he knew that because I didn't give him time to elaborate?" His tone doesn't sound happy. I narrow my eyes at him.

"Not that it's any of your business, but I used to date his brother."

Kane lowers his eyes and just shakes his head. He raises them once again towards me and asks, "Are your parents home?"

I have no idea why I did not lie because I really do not know him, but I shook my head no.

Looking up into his eyes, he steps to me, "Why didn't you come meet me tonight?"

"Yesterday was just too intense for me. Right now is almost too intense for me. I really don't want to deal with whatever this is at the moment."

I hear him chuckle, and I feel it all the way down to my toes.

"I love an honest woman. Hell Jay, you think I want this right now? You have no clue where I'm coming from. I'm trying to build a company with my brother down here and working two jobs. I barely have a moment to breathe. It's crazy because I've been trying to figure out what the hell I am doing in my life, when suddenly, I spot this girl who, in an instant, makes me laugh and I haven't done that in a long time. I'm not looking for anything serious, but I couldn't concentrate last night or today wondering about what would happen when I saw you next. I dreamed of you all night long, and I woke up needing to see you. If I would have known where you lived, I would have been here this morning."

He lifts his arms and cradles my face with his strong hands. I close my eyes and let his voice pour over me.

"I've never burned for a woman before, and all night, I burned for you."

A full tremor shakes my body. I don't have to open my eyes to know that he feels it.

"Look at me, Jay. If I could walk away, I would. I need to walk away, but I can't. Nothing in this world could make me. Shit, it's only been twenty-four hours since we met. This is crazy. You don't know me, but I know you feel this." His eyes plead with mine.

I've lied to everyone these last two years. I've lied to lifelong friends and to my family, but as much as I know that I need to lie to this man and back away from him, I can't. I grab the back of his head and pull his lips to mine and in that instant; we both went up in flames. I actually hear him growl. Our hands are everywhere and he kisses me as he pushes me inside and shuts the door behind us. He backs me up to the round table in the middle of the hall, and lifts me up to sit on it. Not for a moment do his lips leave mine. He kisses a trail from my ear to my neck while I rub my hands up and down his back and then to the front to unzip his jacket.

Kane removes it, and I push my hands underneath his shirt to feel his skin. Sucking in air, he moans, and I pull his shirt up and off. God his chest is beautifully ripped. Grazing my fingers across his nipples, his head falls back, and I immediately start kissing his neck. He tastes divine. He's a wonderful blend of salty and sweet as I lick from one side to the other. Yanking my tank top over my head, he stares at my breasts.

He glances up from my chest and into my eyes with a look of appreciation on his face. He kisses my mouth with a chaste kiss and repeats that kiss to each nipple. Now it is my turn to moan as he feasts on each one. Slowly, he pushes me down with my back on the table, and he crawls on top of me as he kisses my mouth like there is no tomorrow. Rubbing my hips with his, my body is strung tight. Our bodies are in tune with one another, and he senses what I need. He grinds his hips hard into the vee of mine as I shatter. He does that a couple of more times, and I feel his body shudder as he moans, resting all of his weight on top of me.

I'm not sure how long we lay like that. It takes several minutes for our breathing to return to a normal pace. His body is still on top of mine, and as far as I am concerned, I never need to breathe again. I love his weight on me. His head rests on my chest as his hand rubs circles on my stomach.

"I haven't done that since I was a teenager," he says and laughs. "I think I would have went down in flames had I actually been inside of you."

Oh my God, my body lights up again at his words. He finally climbs off the table and grabs my hand to pull me up.

"Baby, where is the nearest bathroom?"

Pointing him to it, I just sit there, grab my tank top off the table, and slowly put it back on. I lower my head to my hands, and the weight of everything that happened crashes over me. What the hell am I doing?

I hop off the table as he walks out of the bathroom. Grabbing his shirt off the floor, I sling it at him. I can't look him in the eyes. I'm embarrassed that I just made out with him like that. I can handle one night stands, but this is different. He is different.

"Um, you have to go. Like right now. I have school in the morning."

I notice him smile as he slides his t-shirt on.

"What time is your first class? I could meet you for lunch."

What the hell is he talking about? I snap at him, "The same time it starts every morning, and we can't leave campus for lunch."

At that moment, I see him flinch, and his eyes get a little bigger.

"Aren't you at the University?"

Looking at him, I roll my eyes. "No, I'm a senior at Jackson Heights High School." Oh no. I watch him step back, and his face looks a little green.

"How old are you, Jay? And, please don't lie."

Okay, that last part pisses me off. I'd been more honest with him tonight, more so than with anyone else in the last two years. Rolling my eyes at him, I say, "You weren't too worried about that when your mouth was all over me a minute ago." I hated to sound crass, but damn, now I am hurt and pissed. "You need to go," I almost shout at him. He grabs me around the waist and pulls me to him.

"Look, I'm sorry if that hurt your feelings, but this is important. Almost everyone I talked to tonight trying to get info on you said how you hung out at the bar. I know you're friends with Jill. I just assumed you were at least twenty-one. My bad, but God Jay, this is so important. I don't want to go to jail if you're a minor."

Looking at him, I ask sarcastically, "So If I tell you I am under eighteen, you are just going to leave? No matter what your feelings are, you would just walk away? Even if I beg you to take me upstairs right this minute?" He looks in pain for about a second, but then he glances into my eyes.

"Yes Jay, I would walk away." He rubs his hand over his head and says, "God, I would hate every single minute, but yeah, I couldn't be that type of guy." I knew he meant it. With a huge sigh, I look at him.

"I turned eighteen last July. My parents held me back a year so that I could go to school with their friends' kids. I have a fake ID that helps me drink when I need to." He looks a little relieved.

"But you're still in high school, huh?"

"Yes Kane. Is that a deal breaker for us?"

He smirks, "It should be, but thank God you're at least legal, and right now, that is good enough for me." He leans down to kiss me, but I pull my mouth back.

"Kane, we need to slow down just a little. We don't know each other, at all really, and I must seem like a super slut after knowing you what, maybe a day?" I bow my head into my hands and continue, "If you want only one night and that's it, then we can go upstairs, but if you really want more, then I need to slow everything down. I need to think about this."

"I get that. I'm not looking for anything serious, Jay, but the thought of not seeing you again? Honestly, it's not sitting well with me. How about I take you to dinner tomorrow? I'll pick you up around seven?"

"Yeah", I reply. He leans to kiss me again, and I turn my cheek. "Kane, I'm not that strong. If you kiss me, I'm not sure I can let you leave," my eyes plead with his. He shakes his head and follows me as I walk to the door. Nothing else is said. Nothing had to be. After he leaves, I climb the stairs and go straight to bed.

I open my eyes to the bright light again. My body is so cold from laying on what seems to be a steel table. My arms and legs are so

31

heavy that I can't seem to move them. A man's voice is coming from the end of the table discussing what golf course he plans to play this weekend. Suddenly, the bright light above me is blocked, and my beautiful dark angel leans down to me. His lips are inches from mine.

"Are you comfy, my love?" He gently kisses my lips, "You're being such a good girl. Just lay there my beautiful whore." A sob is retched from my body, and tears trickle down the side of my face. "Hush, no tears," he whispers, "you're just taking one more step closer to being with me." His tongue sweeps out of his mouth, and it's black and forked like a snake. I can feel it as it traces my lips, trying to invade my mouth.

I wake up screaming and turn to sob into my pillow. It is hours before I finally fall back to sleep.

Chapter Three

I wake before my alarm clock goes off, and I decide to get an early start. I didn't think much about my situation with Kane last night before bed. Honestly, I can't think about it right now either. One day at a time is all I can do, and I need to get through another day of school. The home phone rings, and I rush to answer it, knowing it's one of my parents.

"James, I just want to check on you, sweetie." It's my dad.

"Hey Dad, I'm fine. Everything is good here." The lies roll off my tongue.

"Good. Your mother and I both might be another week getting home. We are taking some time for a little vacation. I just wanted to see if you needed anything."

"That's fine, Dad, I am busy with school anyways."

"Great James, we'll call later this week."

At last there is silence as he ends the call; the same way he ends all of his phone calls.

"Love you too," I tell dead air.

Rushing to get dressed, I decide on my regular school attire with a white denim skirt, light pink tee, and matching Converse shoes. I play with my hair in the mirror and use my big barrel curling iron to style it. It turns out super cute. Mentally, I know I'm dressing thinking about Kane, and a thread of excitement runs through me. I have chosen for the past two years not to have any long term commitments. For the first time in a long time, I'm thinking about letting someone get close, and it scares the hell out of me. On the other hand, I am starved to hold someone for longer than an hour.

With my ear buds in and jamming to my music, I go to get into my car to head to school. When I open the car door, I happen to look up and finally notice the motorcycle parked behind me. The sexiest man alive is sitting on it. Just looking at him, I feel a peace that I haven't felt in a long time. I know in that instant that maybe I don't know him, but it feels like my soul has known his forever. Does it really matter that we don't know everything about each other? The truth is, evil can reside in anyone and most of the time, it is in those we least expect or those we are closest to. Staring at Kane, I think to myself, "The hell with it. I'm going to live my life for me now."

We are both drawn to each other. Ripping the music from my ears, I toss my book bag into the car and put a little extra swing in my hips as I walk towards him. He smiles at me and slides off his bike. I don't hesitate once I reach him. I jump up and wrap my long legs around his waist.

"Miss me?" I ask.

"All night," he says as he kisses me like a ravenous man. He tastes like orange juice, and I could have kissed him all day, but I finally break away.

"I'm going to be late." I attempt to put my legs down, but he wraps me tighter around him.

"One more for the road," he whispers. "Get me through the day." His lips are so soft, and I swear his tongue is ultra-smooth. We kiss like it's our last, and we both moan. I pull away, and this time, he lets me go.

"I can't believe you're here. I wanted to see you this morning." My eyes grow wide; I cannot believe I just said that out loud. He grabs my hands and looks into my eyes.

"Jay, you can't say that to me and expect me to let you walk away."

"Don't leave then. Let's go inside, and I'll play hooky for the day. I want to be with you." I can see how much he wants me.

"Jay, there is nothing I want more, but I have to work. My brother would kill me if I didn't show up. He's going to be pissed that I'm late. It's a big job, and it's huge for our business."

I could tell he is torn, so I put the tip of my finger to his mouth.

"It's okay. Really, I just wanted you to know how I felt."

"God girl, you're going to kill me," he says as he tugs me to him and kisses me once more.

I am late to first period, but, it was worth it. Once I am seated, I look up, and Cal is staring at me. He just smiles at me and leans closer.

"Wow, there's the girl I used to know. I haven't seen you smile like that in years. Whatever it is, keep doing it every morning. Let me know if you need any help making you smile."

The fool actually wiggles his eyebrows at me. I can't help but laugh out loud at him. Then, I notice the silence. The entire class, along with Mrs. Davis, is staring at me with mouths agape. Geez, these people need to get a life. Mrs. Davis begins talking, and Cal leans in close again.

"I need to talk with you after class," he whispers. I nod and turn towards the board.

I forget about talking to Cal when he gets held up by some of the football players after class. Rhye glares at me all through second period like he is pissed, but at least he leaves me alone. By my third period, I start to realize that something was definitely up, and I keep getting the feeling that I was the center of it. I finally catch up to Cal at the beginning of lunch in the cafeteria.

"Do you know what is up with everyone?" Cal hangs his head down, and before he gets a chance to talk, I hear a high pitch scream.

"You bitch, how dare you! He's mine!" I turn just in time to see Cal grab Stacie and pull her away before she slaps me. "You can't have him back," she screams. Coach Sanders grabs her from Cal and proceeds to drag her out of the cafeteria.

"What the hell, Cal? What is she talking about?" I ask.

His cheeks redden as he responds, "Listen, I tried to tell you this morning. JT broke up with Stacie last night and told her it was because you two were getting back together. Everyone was hanging out when it happened, and of course, it was a loud public break up. So pretty much, JT told the whole school you both were back together. Then you come in smiling this morning and well, you can guess what everyone thought."

Speak of the devil. At that moment, JT walks into the cafeteria. Marching straight up to him, I say harshly, "We need to talk," and turn around hoping he follows me. I don't want to have this conversation anywhere near school, so I walk to my car and unlock both doors. I sit down on the driver's side as JT sits down on the passenger side.

"What the hell, JT?"

He turns toward me, holding both his hands up, "Just listen to me for a second, okay? I deserve for you to hear me out. When I talked to you the other day, I could see in your eyes that you still loved me. I don't care what happened in the past. I just know that I need you in my future. The past two years have been the most miserable years of my existence. You left me, God Jay, I was broken. I thought I could drink the pain away, and I tried to replace you. I loved that everyone else started to hate you too. Lately, I'm starting to realize that this whole time, I haven't been moving on, but have been waiting for you to come back to me. I know now I can't live without you." His voice breaks, and tears roll down his face.

Hearing his words killed me. I have loved this boy for most of my life. Pulling JT into a hug, I let us both cry for what was, and what I knew, could never be again.

Lifting my head, I say, "JT, I'm not that same girl you once loved." He tries to interrupt me, but I continue, "I heard you out, so now it's my turn. I'll always love you, but right now I can't be with you."

He grabs both of my arms and doesn't let go, "Just tell me why?

I deserve to know what took you from me."

I shake my head no.

"Damn you," he says. "Just tell me the truth, was there someone that you cheated on me with? I need to know, Jay, and don't you dare lie to me."

I look into his red rimmed eyes and whisper, "No JT, I would never have cheated on you. There was no one I loved more than you."

He tries to pull me toward him but is startled when the passenger door is jerked open. Coach Branch leans in and asks, "Problem here guys?" He notices JT's hands on me and glares at him, "Higgins, maybe you need to head to class, son."

I jump out of the car before JT has time to get out, and I head for the school doors. Coach Branch calls for me, but I do not listen. I only turn back for a second when I reach the school. JT is walking beside him, and neither one is talking.

Running to my locker, I grab my books and head for the front office. My parents had spoken with the school, and because of their work schedule, I am allowed to check myself out if I do not feel well. I didn't do it very often because I didn't want my parents to revoke that status, but today is that kind of day. Driving home, I notice I had missed a text message.

Kane – Hopefully I didn't make you too late this morn

I wait until I get home to text back.

Me – Not much, was your bro mad?

Kane – He'll get over it

Me – Can't wait for tonight!!! What should I wear?

Kane – Something sexy ;)

Me – I can do that. See you at 7.

Kane – See U…btw…I know what they say about candy…and it's not true

Me – ????????

Kane – That it's TOO SWEET…

Me – lol…Glad I like sweets then… ;)

Next, I need to text Cal for help.

Me – Please tell JT that I need some time. Will NOT be at home, going to a friend's house for the night.

Cal – I'll try Jay. What happened??? Coach B is pissed at him and JT isn't talking to anyone. Coach B told Coach S that JT was harassing you and to back off. WTH????

Me – Please help Cal…just keep JT away for now. I'll explain later…K??????

JT and I are over. We can't go back, and I'm not sure we can ever go forward. He would never let the past go. He can't. After two years, why is everything falling apart now?

Leaving the house, I decide I deserve a little pampering and head to the local spa for a manicure and pedicure. I also opt for a blow out and style with big curls loosely placed on top of my head. I arrive home with just enough time to wash off and get dressed. I pick a black dress from my closet. The front was simple and offset with a diamond pendant draped from my neck. The hemline was short, and an ultra-low drop grazed the small of my back. I slip on a pair of killer black heels, light make-up, and tons of lip gloss.

Waiting for Kane to arrive, I wonder how indecent this skirt is going to look on the back of a motorcycle. When the doorbell chimes, I peek through the front door glass and see him standing there. Wow. Kane in a leather jacket and tight blue jeans this morning was sexy as hell. Kane dressed in black dress pants and a gray knit shirt is panty-dropping hot.

When I open the door, he smiles and looks me up and down. Peering deep into my eyes, he says, "Damn, Jay," and pulls me to him. His mouth softly caresses mine, and I feel his tongue tracing my lips. "God, you taste good." His words are whispered into my mouth. He runs his hands down both my arms until they are holding mine. I start to pull him inside, but he hesitates. "Now I'm the one who is not strong enough to come in and be able to leave for dinner. C'mon let's go." He smiles at me, and those dimples make my knees go weak.

I lean into him and kiss the right dimple and then the left. He groans, and I say, "Let me grab my purse." Picking it up from the table, I follow him out the door.

Instead of his motorcycle, there is a silver Chrysler Crossfire in the driveway. "I love your motorcycle Kane, but I really love this," I say looking at the car.

He just smiles and opens the passenger door to help me in. After he sits down, he turns to me and pulls me as far as he can towards him. His body heat radiates to me, and I can almost feel a tangible connection between us. His green eyes stare into mine.

"Did you know your eyes are like molten silver when you look at me?"

"Here I am, thinking how yours are like emeralds," I return in a whisper. I place my hand against his face, caressing his cheek.

He grabs me behind my neck and pulls my lips to his. This kiss soars from zero to sixty in seconds. My body goes up in flames, and I moan. Or maybe it is him. His hands are in my hair, and mine are holding his face. He gently pushes my head back, separating my mouth from his.

"Jay, we are not going to make it to dinner like this." I think I whimper, not in pain, but because I want to taste his mouth again. "Baby, I want to take you out." It's like I am in a haze. I hear him talking to me, but my body is on fire. I have never felt like this. After a minute, I try to pull out of his hold, and he lets me go.

He backs out of the driveway and asks me about what my parents do for a living. I tell him about them, my childhood, and all the trouble Molly, Reed and I used to get into. He talks about growing up and how he and his brother were always super close. His father died when they were teenagers, but his mom is still alive and he wants to move her here.

We arrive at a local Italian restaurant, and before I know it, we are seated and our order is placed. I laugh when I notice the waitress checking him out. I'm sure he gets that everywhere.

"I can't wait to meet your friends."

My heart drops with his statement, and I look down at the table. "I'm not close with them anymore." After a couple of seconds, I look up waiting for him to ask why, but he surprises me and doesn't.

Compassion fills his eyes, "Must have been painful losing them."

"Yeah, I don't like talking about it." He nods and begins telling me more about himself.

The rest of dinner we lightly banter back and forth. After they remove our food, he asks if I want dessert. I reply, "Yes," looking into his eyes, "you."

"Babe."

Just that one word from him accompanied by the smile on his face, and I'm done. He pays for dinner and helps me out of my chair. As we leave, I hear my name and turn to look back at a table in the corner. Coach Branch and his wife are evidently having dinner.

He stands up, "Hey James. You remember James, don't you Lisa?" He asks his wife. She just nods her head and continues to smile at me.

"How are you, James?" She asks.

I look down at her and say, "Fine." My answer must have come out sounding short because her smile dims a little. I turn towards Coach Branch as he speaks.

"Well who do we have here, Jay? Bruce Branch," he says holding his hand out to Kane.

"Kane David," Kane replies while shaking his hand.

Coach Branch cuts his eyes to me. "I didn't know you were seeing anyone?"

"Sorry, we really need to be leaving," I say cutting off his question. I grab Kane's hand and head towards the door, pulling him behind me.

As I rush to make an exit, I let go of Kane's hand and look back briefly to insure he is still behind me. I turn around to open the door and plow into Rhye instead. He puts both his hands on my arms to keep us steady.

"Whoa! Slow down." He rubs his hands up and down my arms, leaning into me. "Looks like you are in a hurry, Jay. Escaping from your date here?" He looks up at Kane behind me, and Kane seems pissed.

Pushing out of Rhye's arms, I tell him, "No, but if I was, it wouldn't be to you."

He laughs and looks at Kane. "She is fiery as shit, and let me tell you, it makes for a great lay."

Kane takes a step towards him, but I grab his hand again and pull him away from Rhye.

"Forget you, Rhye," I say as Kane and I walk outside. We barely make it to his car before he explodes.

"What the hell, Jay? Want to tell me what just happened back there? Who was that first guy and his wife and who the hell was that jack-off at the door?" He clinches his jaw, and his face turns bright red.

Trying not to hyperventilate, I struggle to slow down my breathing. Kane is so pissed about Rhye that I don't think he notices.

"Damn, Jay, when that Branch guy was talking to you, I honestly thought you were going to puke on him. Your face was solid white." He stares at me, waiting for answer.

My voice breaks when I answer him. "He's just a coach at my school."

"Damn, did he fail you in PE or something?" He laughs at his own joke, but when he notices the look on my face, he stops. "What is it, Jay? What is he to you?"

"He is nothing to me," I reply as I turn away from him to get into the car. Kane grabs the door and closes it before I can open it.

"Look at me, Jay. Who was that other guy?"

"An asshole," I say angrily. He watches me, wanting me to say more. I sigh and reply, "He's just a guy that I unfortunately gave the time of day to once, and now wish I hadn't. Look, I don't feel good. Can you please take me home?" Kane begins to speak, but I look at him and interrupt, "Please?" He opens the door, and I slide in.

Kane is quiet the whole ride home. He has Radiohead's, "Karma Police," playing on the radio. I crank it up loud so I don't have to talk to him. As he turns into my driveway, I lower the volume. He puts the car in park but leaves it running. Then, he turns to me.

He starts to say something, but I am quicker. "Kane, my life is so messed up right now. I can't even begin to tell you how much. I know you want answers about the restaurant, but right now, I can't talk about it." Tears begin to fall down my cheeks; I am unable control my emotions. "You don't need this extra drama in your life right now, and I come with a shit load of it. I know you're not looking for anything serious." I open the door to get out, but Kane reaches for my arm and gently pulls me back.

"Jay, you're right, I don't need any more bullshit in my life right now."

I nod in agreement.

"So, that is why you are going to let me help you work some of it out. I am not walking away from what we are starting here, so we will just deal with it." He draws me toward him, "I don't know what it is, but you will tell me all of it–just not tonight." He kisses me lightly on the lips. "I want you, Jay, but I can wait for the right time for us, and I know that's just not tonight." I know he can see the shock on my face. He kisses the tip of my nose and turns to open his door.

After helping me out of the car, he accompanies me to the front door. I unlock it and step inside. When he doesn't follow, I spin back around. "Lock the door and turn the alarm on after I leave. I'll see you in the morning." He kisses me lightly on the lips and walks away.

"Kane," I call to him, and he stops to look at me. "I thought you didn't want anything serious?" His eyes meet mine.

"Yeah, that's what I thought too." He smiles and turns to leave.

Grinning to myself, I close the door and switch on the alarm. My thoughts never leave Kane as I crawl into bed that night and fall asleep.

I was back in the room with the dirty white walls. This time, I am alone. The cold hard metal seat I am sitting on is situated in the middle of the room. Looking down, I have on a hospital gown, but my stomach is flat. I close my eyes tightly when I feel hot air being breathed on the back of my neck. My dark demon is here again.

He gently lifts my hair and continues to nuzzle his nose deeper into the crook of my neck. "I do so love the innocent ones. They always taste the sweetest." I feel him lick my neck, and then his needle sharp teeth sink into my shoulder blade. They pierce my body, and blood starts to run down my arm turning my white gown red. He picks me up and lays me on the floor. I hear him pull his zipper down and feel him push my gown up. The warm blood flows faster down my body. He shifts over me and starts to push into me painfully. I scream as he tears me, and he laughs louder as I cry out for help.

I wake again with balmy tears running down my face and body. Alone in my torment. As I always am.

Chapter Four

I hit snooze the first time I think my alarm is going off the following morning. It feels like just minutes later, and it is going off again. Rolling towards the end of the bed, I slam my hand harder on the snooze button, but the darn thing won't turn off. Lifting my head, I realize it is the doorbell. Damn. It is way too early for this.

The sun is just coming through my windows. I am in a cami and boxers, and I catch a glimpse of my serious bed head in the mirror as I walk down stairs. Whoever is at the door at this hour is going to get me just like this. When I get to the foyer, I see JT standing at the door, looking away. I think for a minute about not answering it, but I quickly realize that if Kane drops by this morning, it could spell disaster. I turn off the alarm and open the door.

"What the hell, JT?" I ask.

He is dressed in his running clothes and looks like he hasn't slept. His eyes travel up and down my body, and I cross my arms over my chest. I am more covered than a bathing suit, but I should have put on a robe.

"Can I come in so we can talk?"

"No, you can't, JT. It is way too early in the morning. Did Cal not tell you I need some time?"

He steps into the doorway in front of me. "I gave you plenty of time. We are working this shit out today. I can't take any more of this, Jay."

"Look, please don't do this. I've thought about it, and we can't go back. You have to let me go," I plead and try to push him back.

He quickly grabs me and pushes me backwards into the house. His grip is tight, and his face is harsh. "Fuck that, Jay! I am getting some damn answers. I'm not that little boy you threw away two years ago."

My heart starts fluttering, and the panic rises fast. He barely shakes my shoulders, but something in me snaps. I start trying to pull away and yell at him, "Let me go, JT! Let me go NOW!" I am shaking, and tears stream down my face while I try to jerk my hands free.

"Jesus, Jay, calm down I just want to talk."

My breath catches in my chest, and I try to kick his shin. He blocks me in an attempt to avoid injury. JT wraps his arms around me, securing my hands, and picks me up.

"Please let me go," I sob as he carries me into the living room and over to the couch. He lays me down and uses his body to pin me to the cushions, securing my hands and feet.

"Quit kicking me, and calm down, Jay! This is ridiculous."

I can't breathe. Every breath is shallow, and my vision starts to waver.

"What the hell? Jay, calm down. JAY!" He is yelling.

I feel him being lifted off of me. From far away, I hear mewling sounds, and I do not realize they are coming from me. The sound of muffled voices drifts over me, but nothing is getting through my head. Just like the last time, the darkness consumes me.

"Wake up, James. Come on, Jay, I need you to wake up for me."

His voice seems miles away. I feel him stroking my face. "Please baby, I don't know what to do. Just wake up."

My eyes flutter open, and my head is in Kane's lap. His eyes are on mine.

"Jay, you okay? Do I need to call the police? Talk to me, please." His voice sounds more hoarse than normal, and his beautiful green eyes are dark with worry.

"I'm good," my voice is weak, "please help me sit up."

As I lean forward, I notice JT sitting on the floor in the corner staring at me. He has several scratches down one cheek, and his face looks like got the hell beat out of him. There is a gash on his forehead, and his nose is swollen and bleeding. His eyes are red, and it looks like he has been crying.

"I am so sorry, Jay," JT keeps repeating in a whisper. He continues staring at me as if he has never seen me before.

"Shut the fuck up," Kane growls at him.

JT closes both of his eyes tightly, and tears stream down his cheeks. When he finally speaks, his voice is shaky. "Who hurt you, Jay? Just name the bastard, and I'll kill him. This whole time, I didn't get it. I knew you would never cheat on me. That answer always bothered me because I knew it wasn't the truth. FUCK," he yells in anguish as he stands up.

Kane pulls me closer in his arms as JT starts toward me. Kane says to him, "That's close enough."

He stops, and tears continue to fall down his face. I do not realize that tears are also streaming down mine until I feel Kane wipe them away. JT drops to his knees again.

"Please, Jay. Just tell me who it was. Oh my God, I think I know what happened! Just tell me. God, I am so sorry. I never thought that would be why. I should have known. I should have known," he cries and bows his head sobbing.

Closing my eyes tightly, I silently pray this is a nightmare and I will awaken at any moment. I feel like I am being stripped bare and shredded to pieces. Is my soul slipping through the slashes of me? I can't allow this to happen. Standing suddenly, I push away from Kane.

"Get out of my house, NOW, both of you. Just get out!" I scream. I know I probably look like a crazy woman, but I don't care at this moment. Looking down at JT, I snarl at him, "Get the fuck out of my house, JT. I don't know what you're talking about, but you can keep your fucking opinions to yourself. You don't know anything about me. Don't you dare breathe a word of what you think 'happened.' Just get out," I scream and dive toward him swinging. Before my hand can make contact with him, Kane grabs and pulls me back. I jerk my body out of his arms and turn towards him, "Leave Kane. Just leave."

Kane looks at me and shakes his head. Standing, he turns to JT, "Man, you need to leave." JT doesn't even look at him. He stands still, continuing to stare at me.

"I am so sorry," he says quietly and turns to walk away.

I hear the front door open and close. My eyes go to Kane, and he's looking at me with pity in his eyes. My breaths are coming fast, and it feels like my heart will erupt from my chest at any moment.

I open my mouth to tell him to leave when he says, "I'm not leaving, so get that out of your fucking head. You can either talk about what just happened or you can just let me hold you." He sits down on the couch and lowers his head to his hands.

"Damn Jay, this morning I walk up to your front door, and it's cracked opened. Then I hear you screaming. So I run in and find a guy holding you down. You fainted, and I totally lost my shit and almost beat that kid to death. He didn't even fight me off. He was worried about you and begged me to make sure you were okay." He looks up at me. "Now, I'm not going to pretend I didn't hear what he said or even pretend I don't know what he might have meant."

I cut him off, "Just shut up. What? You've known me for literally three days. You don't know me at all. Just get out of my house."

He shakes his head and I can tell he wants to argue. Finally, he stands and looks at me, "What the fuck ever." He walks out of the living room and never looks back.

I jump when the front door slams. My knees give out, and I fall to the floor hanging my head. The pain radiates down my body from my heart. It's physical. When will it stop? A thought flashes through my mind, and I realize I can make it stop. Upstairs, in my bathroom closet, sits a bottle of different pills. It's a collection of sorts that I have been gathering for the last year. It would be a lethal combination if taken at the same time.

My thoughts are interrupted when I hear the front door open and close again. I look up as my mother walks into the room. When she sees me on the floor, she rushes forward to grab me.

"Jesus, Jay, what happened? Are you okay? Dale!" she screams for my father.

I lay my head on her shoulder and sob. When was the last time that I had cried to my mom? It had been years. Her hands grip me, and she holds me tightly to her chest.

"It's okay, honey. I'm here." She kisses the top of my head. I hear feet pounding against the floor as my dad runs into the room.

"Paige, what is going on?" He asks my mom as he kneels on the floor next to us. Laying his hand on top of mine, he asks, "James, are you okay?" I can hear the concern in his voice.

Raising my head, I look at them. I have to tell them something. "I'm fine, really. I just had a fight with JT." They look at each other over my head. My dad is the first one to speak.

"A fight with JT? I'm hoping you mean over the phone, James, and not that he was here this early in the morning."

"Dale, leave her alone," my mom says to him. "Jay, I didn't know you and JT were back together?" She holds me away from her and looks at me.

"It's a long story, Mom. Really, I'm okay." Pulling away from her, I wipe the tears from my face, and we all stand up. "What are you guys doing home?"

"We had some last minute issues with the business, and we had to come back to deal with them," my mom replies. "Honey, do you want to talk about anything?" I can see the worry in her and my dad's eyes.

"I'm fine really. It's been a rough first week of school, and I left early yesterday because I didn't feel very well. I'm going to stay home today if it's okay with you?"

My dad starts to shake his head, but my mother lays a hand on his arm and speaks. "That's fine, Jay. I'll call school and let them know. Why don't you go upstairs and lie down. I'll come up and check on you in a minute."

I nod my head and begin to walk away. At the door, I turn and see my parents whispering to each other. I know my parents love me, and I have never doubted that. I just don't think they know what to do with me anymore. I climb the stairs, reach my room, and fall into bed. Pulling the covers over my head, I let myself sink into a restless sleep.

"Jay, wake up sweetie."

My mother's voice wakes me. Her hand brushes through my hair as she sits on the side of the bed. Concern is etched on her face, and pain fills her voice.

"You know if you ever want to talk about anything, I'm here to listen. Your dad and I have been worried about you. I know we don't talk like we used to."

Smiling at her, I answer, "I know, Mom, and really I'm okay. JT and I are just trying to work out our problems. Things just got out of hand this morning. I am so sorry that you and dad had to see me like that."

"No Jay, don't feel that way. We want you to talk to us. You have shut me out the past couple of years, and I don't know how to talk to you anymore."

I don't know what to say to that. It's true. We used to be a lot closer, but my life has changed so much in the last two years. So much has been taken from me.

"Thanks for just being here, Mom. I love you." I sit up in the bed.

"Just know that we are always here for you." She hugs my neck and stands up. "Do you want something to eat? Your dad and I are driving to the office, but I could fix something before we leave."

"I'm good. I'll grab something in a little bit."

"When I know our schedule, I'll let you know. See you sweetie." She kisses the top of my head and walks out.

My phone vibrates on the table beside my bed. I reach over and grab it to read my text messages.

Cal – R u okay???? Why are you not at school??? Did something hap w/JT? Looks like someone beat the shit out of him, but he won't talk about it.

Me – I'm just not feeling well. Please tell JT I'm okay. Make sure he's okay for me.

I shake my head reading the next text and decide to ignore it.

Rhye – I can't get you out up my f'n head… Shouldn't have said that last night at the restaurant. Can we just talk? Did you hear your song the other night?

It is sunny outside, so I shower, shave my legs, and head outs to lay by the pool for the day. I slip my ear buds in and turn on some music. My thoughts are running wild about what I am going to say to Kane. He probably doesn't even want to talk to me anymore. I wouldn't blame him. After a while, my phone vibrates against me.

Kane – R U at school?

Me – No…I stayed at home. My parents are here.

Kane – K

Me – ??????

I'm not sure where he is going with this. I want to know if he still wants to see me again.

Me – Did you want to come over and talk?

Kane – Now you want to talk? No Jay, I don't want to talk. I just wanted to make sure you were okay.

Me – I am sorry about this morning…

He never texts back. I go inside later that afternoon to freshen up and lay back down. Closing my eyes, I figure I can sleep my life away.

When I wake again, it is dark outside. I walk downstairs and hear my parents talking in the kitchen. My father's voice keeps getting louder.

"I'm worried about her, Paige. She never has friends over anymore. Dan and Sandra have told us both that she still doesn't speak to Molly. This has gone on long enough. Now all of the sudden JT is back in the picture. I don't think this is a good thing. Has she even applied to any colleges? She doesn't talk to anyone anymore."

"Calm down, Dale. When she is ready, she will talk to us. You can't push her." I can tell that my mom is trying to calm him down.

"When she is ready? It's been two years. We have let things go and given her time to come to us. She hasn't, and her future is at stake."

"We need to give her a little more time. She is coming around," my mother tells him.

Not wanting to hear anymore, I walk into the kitchen. They stop talking immediately and turn towards me.

"You okay, Jay?" My mom asks.

"I'm fine guys. What are we having for dinner?"

My mother looks at my father, and he turns toward me to answer, "Sorry sweetie. We both have flights out to pick up clients. Some last minute charters." He glances at my mom and then back at me. "Jay, we can cancel them if you need us here."

I don't ever remember my dad offering to cancel business for me. Walking over to him, he opens his arms, and I step into them. Hugging him hard, I say, "Thanks Dad, but I'm good. Everything is fine. I just had a moment this morning. You know, teen angst and all that." I laugh, and it sounds fake even to me, but I can tell that they both buy it.

My mother comes over and hugs me toward her. "You know we are only a phone call away."

"I know, Mom. I'm just going to order a pizza and call it a night. Love you guys."

I slip out of the kitchen before they can say anything else to me. An hour later, they come into my room to tell me goodbye and kiss me before they leave. I still have not heard from Kane. I guess that is that. Grabbing a book that I started last week, I read until I fall asleep.

My alarm clock wakes me early the next morning. Yawning, I realize that I'm not going to be able to get out of school today. Dressing in tan shorts and a gold blousy shirt, I slide on a pair of new metallic sandals and check myself out in the mirror. Yesterday's tanning session was much needed. My skin glows. I leave my hair loose and head down stairs.

I decide to forego the coffee this morning since I didn't set the automatic timer. Grabbing my keys and book bag, I head to school. As I walk out the front door, I hope to see Kane waiting for me. He isn't there, and I should have known better than to even think about it. He's done with me. I can't blame him, though. Even I get tired of my own drama.

Cal is waiting for me next to my parking space when I pull in. He is going to want answers, and I don't have any for him.

"Whatever you're going to say, can you please just save it? Please?" I plead with him. Cal shakes his head.

"We have to talk about our boy eventually, Jay. You know that, right?"

I nod at him. He turns around and walks towards the school building. Taking a deep breath, I follow him to homeroom. Cal sits on one side of the room where there are no more seats, so I sit on the other.

I catch Cal looking at me, but he quickly shifts his eyes down to his desk. He doesn't look at me again during class, but that can't be said about everyone else. They kept glancing and whispering all through the morning. I could ask Cal what they are saying, but I really don't care to know. I could only pray that JT kept his opinions to himself.

I am working on a painting during art class when a shadow falls over my portrait. I look up to see Reed standing there.

"You okay, Jay?"

I immediately glance to where Molly is sitting, and she is staring back at us. Looking up to Reed, I reply, "I'm fine Reed."

My answer comes out a little short, and he winces. For the first time in years, I do not want to be this way toward him. He starts to turn away as I grab for his hand, and he looks back at me. "Thanks for asking," I say and smile at him. I let go of his hand, and he turns to walk away.

My last period is the one I worry about the most because I share it with JT. However, once I arrive in the gym, I hear that he and most of the other football players are out on the football field. They are practicing for next Friday's first game of the season. At least I wouldn't have to deal with him.

After the final bell rings, I walk out to my car and groan when I see the white piece of paper stuck under my windshield wiper. Part of me doesn't want to read it, but then there is that sick sadistic part that needs to see what he'll type next. I grab the note and open it.

I missed you yesterday. I dream about you. Do you have sweet dreams about me?

My breath catches in my lungs. I look around to see if anyone is watching me. Is he watching me? There are so many students walking to their cars and hanging out in the parking lot. I toss it to the ground and get into my car. As I am trying to calm down, my car door jerks open, and Rhye stands there staring down at me.

"Can we talk?"

I grit my teeth and reply, "We have nothing to talk about. I'm done with you, Rhye." I push him away and try to close the door, but he tugs it back open.

"Damn, Jay, just try to listen to me for a couple of seconds. I really shouldn't have said that the other night, but when I saw you with that guy, I just went a little crazy," he says

"Leave me alone," I yell and am finally able to push him away. Pressing the lock button, I start my car up and drive away.

I go straight home, and I do not check my phone until I get there. My heart hurts when I see there are still no calls or text messages from Kane. It's hard to believe that I only met him a week ago. Can you miss someone that you don't really know? I go up to my room and fall across my bed.

When I close my eyes, I see him clear in my mind. I imagine feeling his hard chest underneath my fingers. No guy that I had been with had a body like his, but I think about more than just his body. I want to get to know him better. Hell, I just want to hear his voice. Listening to him talk the other night gave me chill bumps. He probably never wants to see me again, and I can't blame him.

The last two years, I have fought for control of my life. I used sex to control it, and I never opened my heart to another relationship. I said who and when. That way, I could walk away and keep my secrets to myself; however, I also walked away alone. So what am I doing with Kane? He doesn't want a relationship; or does he? Do I? I'm not so sure anymore. I've kept my secret this long. Can I keep them forever and live with them?

"Damn," I yell into the empty room. "Screw this", I think to myself as I roll off the bed and walk into my bathroom to shower. After getting cleaned up, I decide to go out. This is my life, and I decided last year to live it up while I'm here. I curl my hair and put on a little make up. Walking into my closet, I grab my favorite little black dress and a pair of black sling backs. Spraying my body down with a coconut body mist, I smile at the reflection in the mirror. It's funny because I'm starting to see the girl I once was, and I thought she was long gone. Glancing once more in the mirror, I turn and run down the stairs and out to my car.

Driving downtown doesn't take long this evening. I automatically pull into the parking lot of O'Malley's. It is Friday night, and I'm not sure if Kane is working tonight or not. Either way, I am going in. I flash my ID to the bouncer outside, and he smiles letting me through. The bar is always crazy after nine no matter what day of the week it is. With it being the start to the weekend, it is jammed packed mostly with the college crowd. I make my way to the bar and am glad to see Jill is working. She smiles at me as I sit down on a stool.

"What up, girlie? Are you meeting up with Kane tonight?"

I cut my eyes at her and say, "No, I guess you can say it didn't work out. Jill, please do me a favor and not mention it. I've had a shit week. I'm just here to have a good time tonight."

Jill stares at me for a second and nods. "You want the usual?"

I nod back to her. She pours my Jack and Coke and sits it down in front of me. Turning away from the bar, I look around and notice Kip playing pool with some of his buddies. There are a couple of people already on the dance floor. When I start to turn back around, I notice a guy at the end of the bar staring at me. He has shaggy dirty blond hair and is dressed in a dark suit. He dips his chin at me, noting that I am looking at him. Turning back to the bar, I see that Jill is watching me.

"I don't know about that one. He just showed up tonight. Part of the work crowd, not the college." She glances at the guy at the end of the bar. Following her eyes, I see that he is still staring at us. I smile back at him, and he stands up to walk towards me.

"Kyle Larson," he says as he reaches for my hand.

"Jay," I reply back. He kisses the top of my knuckles, and his eyes never leave mine.

"Would you like to dance, Jay?"

I stand and say, "Sure."

He leads me to the dance floor, and a slow song starts to play. He pulls me close to him, and we move together. His hands rub my back but soon start to move elsewhere. I close my eyes and try to let the music just take me, but for the first time in years, it mattered who I was dancing with. I can't relax. The music moves to something faster, and we continue dancing. I turn in his arms with my back facing his front. His hands grip both sides of my hips and touch the flesh below my dress.

I happen to choose that moment to look up across the room and see that Kane is staring back at me. He must have just walked into the bar. My heart races as I notice how good he looks wearing dark jeans and a red polo shirt. At his side is a guy that looks like an older version of him but with a completely shaved head. The guy at his side points toward the bar, and it breaks his intense gaze from me as they head that way.

Turning my body towards Kyle, I continue to move to the music against him. Sweat pours down both of us.

Kyle whispers in my ear, "Let's get something to drink."

Nodding my head, we both walk to the bar hand in hand. I guide us to the opposite end of the bar from Kane. Jill is talking to him but stops when she sees me, and then heads our way.

Kyle looks at me but speaks to Jill, "Line us up with some Patron shots." Jill did as he instructed, and once all six shots were in front of us, she speaks quietly to me.

"Hope you know what you are doing."

I shake my head and tell her the truth, "I haven't known what I have been doing for years." I look at Kyle and lift my first shot to him and drink deep. In minutes, I had finished the other two. Kyle starts laughing and finishes his shots. He grabs my hand to lead me back to the dance floor.

We dance for several songs. I had gotten a pretty good buzz and am finally enjoying myself. The band came on stage and the dance floor became packed. Glancing around, I notice Kane and I guess it is his brother, playing pool with several girls gathered around them. Sweat pours down my hairline and across my chest.

Kyle's mouth is suddenly on my neck, and I don't like it. I pull away, but he grips my body tighter. I push away from him, but he laughs, shakes his head, and tries to pull me closer. I can feel the panic coming over me, but before I am able to react, another arm wraps around my waist and pulls me gently back. Kyle is staring behind me when I hear Kane's voice in my ear.

"Jay, is this douchebag bothering you?" I can tell Kyle can hear him.

"No problems here. We were just dancing, but I guess we're done," Kyle replies back and turns around to walk away.

The music changes to something slow and sexy. I turn around in Kane's arms to face him. His jeweled eyes are piercing, and he isn't smiling. My arms automatically move up and around his neck. We start dancing, never taking our eyes off each other. I have never been more aware of another human being as I am in this moment. He grips me harder by my hips and pulls me closer to him. I finally close my eyes and rest my head on his shoulder. He sings softly in my ear. Shivers run down my body, and I sigh against his neck. I can feel his body tighten against me. When the song ends, he pulls back and looks at me.

"I am so pissed at you, Jay."

"You'll get over it," I say.

He laughs and shakes his head. "Yeah I guess I will. Come on. I want to introduce you to my brother," he says as he pulls me through all the bodies on the dance floor and over to the pool tables. When we get closer, I watch his brother turn towards us.

"So this must be Jay," he states and continues, "Nice dance moves." He laughs to himself. Kane looks at me and shrugs.

"Shut up, Cole. Jay, this is Cole. Cole, this is Jay."

I glance back at Cole and say, "Hi." Kane sits down on a stool and pulls me to sit on his lap.

Cole racks up the balls for another game and says, "So my brother tells me you are a senior in high school." A smirk appears across his face. I guess this is funny to him. "Girls sure didn't look like you when I was in high school."

"Cole," Kane warns. His eyes glare hard at his brother.

"What? I'm just saying your girl is fine, brother. A little young, but at least legal." He laughs. I can tell that Kane is getting pissed. He clenches his jaw.

Cole bends over the pool table, breaking the balls with the cue stick as he turns to me again. "What are your plans for college?"

"I don't have any at the moment," I say to him. It always shocks people when you tell them that, and Cole is no exception.

"So what, you're not going to college?"

"I have no long term plans at the moment. We'll see how everything goes." I can tell he doesn't like my answers, but before he could ask anything else, I turn to see Kip heading my way. Kip looks pissed as he walks right up to me.

"What the hell, Jay? JT is a fucking mess. Did you know that coach almost benched him for the first game this coming Friday because he won't tell anyone who beat the shit out of him? Coach even called our parents, and they have his ass on lock down. I know it has something to do with you, so don't lie. When I tried to talk to him, he just mentioned that something had gone down at your house. Is this the fucker that beat the shit out of him?"

Kip glares at Kane behind me. I can feel Kane's body tense beneath mine. Kip is a big guy, but he has nothing on Kane. Kane pushes me from his lap to stand up. I need to diffuse the situation and fast.

"Listen Kip, JT and I had a misunderstanding. We were fighting and Kane mistook the situation. It wasn't his fault. He thought JT was hurting me."

Kip keeps glaring at Kane. I hear Cole chuckle behind me, and he opens his big mouth.

"Dude, you really don't want any of my little brother. The boy can fight. I do like to be entertained though, and someone trying to kick his ass is always funny."

I glare at Cole because he isn't helping the situation.

Kip turns toward me and says, "You know that JT would never hurt you. He fucking loves you, Jay. It's always been just you for him forever, but he's going to fuck up his football scholarship if he doesn't get his shit together. Don't let your stuff bring him down, whatever it is."

I stare at Kip for a couple of seconds. I've seen him out several times over the past couple of years. He has never really brought JT up, so I am shocked that he is saying anything now.

"Kip, he came to my house and forced his way in. I have told him repeatedly that we are over."

He shakes his head at me, "You know you'll never be over until you give him closure. Can you not just give him that, Jay?" Shaking his head, he turns to walk away.

I can see Cole out of the corner of my eye, staring at me. He looks like he is trying to figure out what or who his brother has gotten involved with. Turning toward Kane, I glance up at him.

"It's late, and I've got to go. I'll talk with you later." I start to walk away, but he pulls me back to him.

"You've been drinking. I'll drive you home in your car, and Cole can follow us." He isn't asking.

"Okay, thanks."

Kane and Cole follow me out of the bar. Kane says something to his brother then heads towards me as Cole walks the other way. Neither of us says anything to each other. When we reach my car, I give him the keys, and he opens the door for me to get in. We pull out, and I notice Cole is following behind us.

"Thanks for driving me home."

He nods his head and turns on the radio. Coldplay fills the silence. I look out the window and think about what Kip said.

"How long have you and that guy's brother been broken up?" His voice is low.

"For about two years." He turns his head towards me with surprise on his face.

"Two years? How long were you with him?"

"Since we were in middle school, I guess. He was my first and only boyfriend pretty much."

"Are you ready to tell me why you guys broke up?"

"Not really. No one knows, Kane. I don't ever talk about it." I turn away and look out the passenger side window.

We drive the rest of the way in silence. He pulls into my driveway and turns the car off. I look back and see Cole pull in behind us. We both get out at the same time, and he walks around to where I am standing. I start to tell him goodnight when he gently cradles my face with his hands and forces me to look into his eyes.

"You pissed me off tonight. I was just telling my brother about you over dinner, and then we walk into the fucking bar and you're on the dance floor with another guy."

"I figured you wised up and decided to drop me like a bad habit," I reply sarcastically.

"I should, but for some crazy reason, I can't get you out of my head. I wasn't going to call you all weekend to give us both some space. I'm trying to slow everything down for you and give you time, but you've got to be on the same fucking page. You frustrate the hell out of me. I'm working the next two nights at the bar. Next Friday night, we are going on a date. I'll pick you up at seven." It wasn't a question.

Looking into his eyes, I am his. "I'll be ready at seven."

He grins at me and says, "Good girl. I'll train you yet." He laughs as I punch him in the arm. He leans down and presses his lips against mine. It is just a simple kiss, but it ignites my body. I open my mouth and let his tongue touch mine. It is over before it gets really good because Cole choose that moment to honk his truck horn.

Kane pulls away, and I see him throw his arm up and shoot his brother a not-so-friendly hand gesture. "I'll call you tomorrow," he says and walks to the truck.

Walking in the house, I lock the door behind me and set the alarm. My mind goes over what Kip said as I shower and fall into my bed. JT needs more from me about what happened, but I just can't go there. I have never talked to anyone about it. For one, so much time has passed that I don't think anyone would believe me. When it first happened, I blamed myself, and then the next month was a nightmare. I just want to forget about it. He ruined me for JT. I was saving my virginity for him. JT and I had been talking about taking our relationship further, and he loved the thought that we both had never been with anyone else. Then I was ruined. I fell asleep again with tears in my eyes.

The clock on the wall ticks loudly in my ear. I am in my white room again, however, now crimson blood leaks from the top of the walls running swiftly down to the floor. About a foot of blood pools at the bottom. I sit in the middle of the room directly in the thick liquid and the blood coats my naked legs and backside. My hands twirl through the thick crimson fluid at my side. I can smell the musky scent it has.

Directly in front of me, the thick red liquid starts bubbling, and then something begins rising. I realize it is a head with the hair slicked back from the blood. Next, there are eyes as red as rubies. They stare at me, and the head moves with an almost snake like grace back and forth. Then comes his broad shoulders, and the blood runs down to his flat stomach. He is naked, and when the next part of his body rises, I turn my head. I can see his legs from the corner of my eye, and then he is finally standing whole in front of me.

He drops to his knees and grins. "Come to me," he commands. I shake my head signaling no. "Well, then fight me because I can always take what I want." He grabs my arms as he pulls me to him and tries to kiss my mouth. "Fight me, my beauty. Force always makes it sweeter." I open my mouth to scream.

Sitting up in bed, I notice the sun has started to rise. My body starts to shake as I pull my knees towards my chest, hugging them close. My nightmares are getting darker. I hadn't had one for months until last week. Going back to school has triggered them along with seeing him again. Last year, he left me a couple of notes, but he didn't approach me. Why all of a sudden is he harassing me more?

I can't go back to sleep, so I go ahead and get up. Throwing on my bathing suit, I walk downstairs to grab some breakfast. After eating some toast, I head outside to the pool. The sun is shining bright by the time I lay down on the chair. Not a cloud is in the sky. I turn on my iPhone to my Kings of Leon playlist and close my eyes.

About an hour later, my phone chimes that I have a text message.

Kane – You up?

Me – Soaking up the sun by the pool…want to join me???

Kane – I need to go work-out.

Me – Have fun working out. ☺

Groaning to myself, I guess he is not going to push me. I know it's what I want, but then again, I hate it. The thought of seeing him in his swim shorts warms me all over. Sitting up, I grab the tanning oil and rub it on my skin. The sweet smell of coconut fills the air. Thirty minutes later, my phone chimes again.

Kane – I should be working out…

Me – So why aren't you????

Kane – Because I'm standing at the gate to your pool. I guess I just can't stay away.

I jump off the lounge chair and rush to open the gate. When it swings open my jaw drops. Kane is standing there in his swim shorts, flip flops, and nothing else. My mouth waters at the sight of his chest. My eyes finally go to his, and that's when I laugh. He is staring at my body the same way I am staring at his. Glad I wore my new yellow bikini.

"Like what you see, sweetheart?" I say throwing his words back at him. He laughs, and I know he is remembering that's what he asked me when we first met.

"Yeah, I really like what I see." He grabs me and pulls me towards him for a kiss. "You're all slippery, and you smell so good. Like a tropical island." He kisses my nose and my mouth. "Damn, I can't stay away. I didn't sleep well again last night, and I blame you." I kiss him back and pull away to hold his hand as I lead him to the lounge chair next to mine.

"Now lie down and rest," I say as he plops down on his stomach. Pouring some tanning oil onto my hands, I begin to massage his back. His groan lets me know he likes it. I knead his shoulders and back. Finally, I'm able to read the script across his neck. It reads, "*To Thine Own Self Be True.*" The words hit me hard as I trace the letters with my finger.

My hands rub his lower back and then move down his legs. About twenty minutes later, I finish and move up to kiss his cheek. He is sound asleep. Smiling, I move to my chair and lie down. He really is beautiful, and it seems like it is inside and out. How could I ever let him go? I close my eyes and bask in the warm sun.

The buzzing of a bee above me wakes me up. The sky had turned cloudy, and I look next to me. Kane is sound asleep still on his stomach. His back is red from falling asleep in the sun. I jump up to wake him.

"Wake up, Kane," I say as I shake his shoulder. He leans up and grimaces from the pain of his back. Grabbing my phone, I notice it is almost four in the afternoon.

"Damn, how long did we sleep?" He is still groggy, but he looks so freaking sexy.

"Long enough Sleeping Beauty." I say and grin at him. "Come inside so I can put some aloe on your back. Thank God, that it is cloudy or you would have been really sun burned." He follows me into the kitchen, and I grab the aloe from the fridge."

"That feels so good, Jay." I finish and wash my hands in the sink. He comes up behind me and kisses the back of my head. I close my eyes and feel his mouth drift over my neck and back. "You taste so good. When I'm not with you, all I do is think about you, and when I'm finally with you, I think about when I can be with you again. Crazy, huh?"

Words had left me, so I nod my head yes.

"You make me crazy, Jay." His lips continue down the center of my back. His hands are gripping the sides of my hips.

His lips and hands suddenly leave me, and I turn my head to look back at him. His eyes are shining, and I look down to see that I'm not the only one turned on. His breathing is heavy, and he's now holding onto the kitchen counter like it's a life line.

"You test my patience. I've got to get ready for work. Are you coming to the bar tonight?"

"I think I'll stay around here," I say as I turn towards him.

"I'll be working, so that's good for me. I'd hate to watch all the douchebags hitting on you all night."

"Oh please, Kane, what about all the little college girls worshiping at your feet?" He finally steps back to look at me.

"It's you that I'll be thinking about. I can come here after work if you want me to, but Jay, I think I really should give you a little space. They're ten million things I need to do tomorrow, and I really need to hit the gym. How about I call you tomorrow before I go to work?"

I sigh and answer him, "I guess you're right." I lean in and kiss him. Our lips explore each other for several minutes before I pull back. His eyes are still closed, and he looks so yummy that I lean back in and lightly kiss his lips again.

"I'm going to need the coldest shower when I get home." He and I laugh. I walk him out to his car, and he kisses me one last time. "I'll call you," he says.

"I'll be waiting," I reply. He gets in and drives away. My face feels like it's stretched with the biggest smile. He just makes me happy. I go back in and settle down for a lazy weekend.

The night passes and so does the next day. My parents call and check in with me to make sure everything is fine. Sunday night, Kane calls before work. He tells me that he misses me, and I tell him I'm glad. He laughs at me, promising to call the next day after school. I didn't have any nightmares either night.

Chapter Five

Monday morning arrives with me feeling refreshed and ready for the day. It has been a long time since I have felt this way. Feeling good about myself, I decide to wear my new pale pink sundress to school. It has sweetheart sleeves, and the hem falls just above my knee. I brush my hair until it shines and slide on a new pair of flats. I take a picture of myself blowing a kiss to the mirror and send it to Kane along with a quick text.

Me – Missing you…

Within minutes my phone vibrates back.

Kane – damn baby you look fine…miss you too

I arrive at school early that morning. Walking down the hallway, the school spirit is thick in the air with the opening football game this Friday night. Welcome to the South, where football gods reign supreme. I'm still not sure how to handle JT. First things first, I need to make sure that he hasn't spoken about the other morning to anyone.

Strolling down to the cafeteria, I hope to catch him eating breakfast. When I walk in, he just happens to be walking out. The bruises on his face are turning a light green, and the scratches I made are scabbed over. He is also sporting two black eyes.

I touch his arm and ask, "Hey, can we talk?" His blue eyes are heavy with sadness.

He nods his head and replies, "Sure." I follow him outside the cafeteria building to sit on some lunch benches.

Sitting down, he crosses his arms and ankles. He won't look at me and just hangs his head. I notice that everyone that walks by glances our way. Leaning in, I lower my voice.

"I'm sorry about the other morning. I just wanted to check on you and make sure you are okay."

He looks up at me and says, "I would never have hurt you, Jay. You've known me almost your whole life. I just wanted you to sit still long enough to think about us, but all of a sudden, you went berserk. Did you realize what you were saying while you were fighting me? You kept saying, not again, please not again. You scared the shit out of me, and then your new boyfriend comes running in, thinking I'm attacking you and starts whaling on me."

I can't listen to any more of this. "I don't want to talk about it, JT. Not ever. I am begging you to never make me."

He went to touch my arm, but at the last second, pulls his hand back. I can tell he is terrified to have any contact with me. I continue in a hushed whisper, "You have to move on. You have to let go of us and what happened. Just concentrate on getting your football scholarship."

He grunts, "Not you too? That's all I hear from Coach Branch- that I need to leave you alone and concentrate on football."

I don't want to talk about anyone else. "You have to move on," I plead with him.

"Like you have moved on, Jay?"

"Yes JT, like I'm trying to." That is about as honest as I could get.

He gasps and lowers his head closer to me and says, "I need to know what went down that night. Give me the truth, and I then I can move on." I jerk back ready to tell him the same statement I have always said, but he stops me before I can. "No more lies. Just the truth, for once. If you really want me out of your life, tell me what happened."

I shake my head back and forth and whisper, "No."

JT stands up and turns back to me. His body is shaking, and the pain in his eyes is visible. He leans in close to me and through gritted teeth says, "Someone hurt you and took you away from me. You weren't some girl that I didn't know. You were my world. The reason I smiled every morning when I woke up. I have gone to bed for the last two years remembering how you felt in my arms and how your lips tasted. I looked at you and saw my future. These last two years have been hell for me. If you don't want me back, then fine. I guess I'll have to live with that, but I deserve to know why and who ruined that for me. So unless you can tell me the truth, we have nothing more to say."

He turns around and leaves me sitting there. I'm not sure how long I sit staring at nothing. I am jerked out of my thoughts when I hear a voice behind me.

"Well Miss Stevenson, it was nice meeting your new boyfriend the other night." Coach Branch stands looking at me. He has a football in his hands, juggling it back and forth. He steps closer and continues, "However, my wife and I think he might be a little too old for you. Not to mention he looked like he could be a little rough. I don't want you to get hurt."

I hold my breath, hoping he would walk away. I am always so anxious around him. Stepping even closer, he fumbles the ball out of his hands and it hits me square on my chest. He reaches for it and his hand grazes my breast. I take a swift breath in.

"Goodness, I am so sorry. The ball just slipped out of my hands," he says not looking one bit apologetic.

I jump away when the warning bell rings.

"James, you need to get to class," a soft feminine voice says to me. I turn to see Miss Kell watching us. She almost looks upset, and her eyes volley between Coach Branch and me.

"Yes Ma'am."

"Have a nice day, James," he says to my back, and I never turn around.

I walk straight to my first period class. Cal is waiting for me at the door.

"You are one hard woman to get in touch with. What the hell have you done to JT now? He just shoved me against the wall when I tried to ask him a question."

I walk right by him into the classroom and say, "Let it go, Cal." I sit down, and he sits down beside me. The bell rings, but evidently Mrs. Davis isn't ready to start class yet.

"He's a walking zombie out on the football field. He's got to get his head in the game or we are going to lose on Friday," he says.

I notice that everyone is exceptionally quiet and paying more than enough attention to our conversation. I whisper back to him, "What do you want me to do Cal? I can't give him what he wants. I'm sorry, but I can't." Tears burn my eyes and blur my vision. I can't allow these emotions because I am so afraid if I start crying, I will never stop.

Cal grabs my hand and begs, "Tell him that you'll come and support him this Friday."

"That's not what he wants Cal. Plus, I have a date this Friday," my shaky voice replies.

"I'm not saying as a date, just as a friend. Tell him you'll come and watch him play."

"I'll think about it."

Class finally begins, and we don't say anything else to each other. I don't see JT the rest of the day; however, I do think about what Cal said. My mind is numb. Cal doesn't know what JT wants, and I do not know what to do.

When I arrive home, Kane sends me a text.

Kane – Want to come work out with me tonight? Come downtown to the gym at 6:30.

Me – Sure...I'll see you then.

I set my phone on the kitchen counter and walk out to the pool. I sit down on a lounge chair, and the sun gently warms my face. I close my eyes. Thoughts run through my mind. What am I going to do about JT? How am I supposed to fix him, when I can't even fix me?

As I lie there, I hear my name being called from the back gate. I know that voice immediately. It is the same voice that had shared all of her secrets since we were kids. I unlock and open the door to see Molly standing there. Her fiery red hair is pulled back in a ponytail, and she has on a cute maxi dress. She smiles at me.

"So is bitch season officially over?"

In that moment, I just want to wrap my arms around her and admit how much I have missed her. Struggling with the quiver in my voice, I look back at her.

"It was a long season."

"Ready to talk about it?" Molly has never been one to beat around the bush. We walk over to the chairs, and she sits down next to me.

I hadn't talked to Molly in almost two years, not since the day after everything unraveled. I remember waking up that morning in the shower. The water had eventually lost its warmth, and I don't think I had even noticed when it turned cold. My naked body shook from the chill, and my teeth clicked together loudly. I had bit down on my tongue, and the taste of copper filled my mouth.

Slowly, I stood and groaned at the soreness between my legs. I made myself walk out of the shower, not even drying my body, and glare into the mirror. Silent tears rolled down my face. There were dark purple hand prints on my arms and thighs. Two sets of teeth marks surrounded both of my nipples.

As I stared at the stranger in the mirror, I wondered why her body wasn't more broken. Shouldn't the skin be more mangled and torn? I was instantly angry with her. Why didn't she look as bad as I feel? She still had her skin. She was still protected. I hated her. Didn't she understand what her pretty face and pretty hair had gotten her? Before I knew what I was doing, I picked up my brush and hurled it at the mirror. Glass shattered everywhere. Shards flew down to my feet and nick scratches along my legs.

Now her image matched mine. The body was jagged and mismatched in the broken reflection. I don't know how long I stood there. My legs shook from standing still for so long. My eyes never left the girl in the mirror or what was left of her. I barely made it to my bed before my legs gave out. I climbed in and buried my entire body underneath the covers.

My parents had been out of town and were not due back for another two days. I was supposed to be at school because it was a Friday. It was the second week of my sophomore year. I remember my home phone and cell both ringing for the next several hours. I'm pretty sure I heard the doorbell chime and someone must have been knocking on my front door. I forced all memories out of my head. Nothing seems real.

Molly's voice floats from the hallway. I had forgotten she had an emergency set of house keys and also knew the alarm code. She walked into my room.

"Jay, where the hell were you last night and today? You were supposed to meet Reed and me for pizza after cheerleading practice. JT freaked because you didn't call him either. He couldn't leave school today to check on you, so here I am."

In that moment, I knew I didn't want her to know what happened. No one ever had to know. I pulled the covers down and stared at her. When I spoke, my voice was hoarse. "I'm sick, Mols. Must be the flu or something? You don't want to be here to catch this so you should probably leave."

"Damn Jay, you look bad. Should I take you to the doctor?" Molly looked scared for me.

"I'm fine. Just need to sleep. Tell JT, he doesn't want to catch this bug and I'll call him tomorrow." I pulled the cover back over my head and let the dark envelop me.

"Just call me if you need me. Love you, Jay." I heard her muffled voice say, and then the door closed. I knew she would tell JT that I was sick.

I heard the click of her shoes go down the stairs and out the door. What am I going to do about Molly and Reed? They would know instantly that something is wrong. Oh my God, I didn't know how I would face JT. I was ruined for him. He would never understand what happened. I knew I could go to the police, but then everyone would have to know. I'd seen the T.V. shows where the girl goes to the hospital. NO. No, I didn't want to deal with that.

He got what he wanted. I had been begging for it he said. Wasn't it just a few days earlier that I was flirting with him in P.E. at school? God, I did flirt with him. It was my personality, but everyone knew I was JT's girl. Like the rest of the school, I thought he was super cute. I remember him sending secret smiles during the day at me, and I never thought anything of it.

The more I thought about it, I knew that he was right. No one would ever believe me. He would leave me alone now. We could go on as if nothing happened. Just not as before. I would keep this secret from everyone. I could be strong and put this behind me, but I would have to let Molly, Reed, and JT go. They would guess instantly what had happened. It would be better for everyone.

Making myself get out of bed, I dressed in my sweats. Walking towards the bathroom, I stopped myself before stepping on all the shards of glass that covered the floor. I would have to clean this up before my parents got home and tell them I accidently broke it. Later as I swept the glass away, I could see my reflection in the bigger pieces. That girl was taken away with the trash.

The sound of Molly's voice breaks my thoughts and brings me to the present, "Jay, I miss you. Reed misses you."

Finally, the tears start rolling down my face, and I hang my head. I have really missed them too. Molly grabs me and wraps her arms around me. My body begins to shake from the sobs, and for the first time, I cry and let my burdens go. Molly just holds me and strokes my back.

"I'm so tired, Mols. I'm just so damn tired," I cry. We sit huddled together and eventually my body stops shaking from the sobs. We watch the sun set in silence, and my head rests on Molly's shoulder.

Finally she speaks, "I was so mad at you when you wouldn't talk to me. I thought we told each other everything, and suddenly, you wouldn't let me in. Mad really doesn't describe it. You shut me out. You shut Reed out. You killed JT. I hated you more when you started being bitchy to everyone and stopped hanging around us. I was so stupid not to stop and think that something could have happened to make you act like that."

My body freezes. All I can think is that JT must have talked to her.

Molly continues speaking, "I've been thinking about that lately. That first month you had the flu and were out of school so much that I didn't see you. We would all come to your house, and you refused to see us. Then when we would talk about how you were such a bitch. I think it was easier for Reed and me to hate you because we had each other. We could convince ourselves that you thought you were too good for us, but what you did to JT demolished him. I know now we should have all known better, but hell Jay, we were all hurt."

She stops talking when her voice chokes up. I can't stand it anymore. My world of control that I had worked so hard to build is crumbling around me. My body and mind are exhausted. I let out a sigh and told her what I could.

"Molly, I can't talk about what happened. Not now, maybe not ever, but I miss you. God, I miss talking to you and Reed so much. So many times over the last two years, I've automatically picked up the phone to tell you both something and then realized I couldn't. Right now, I'm so fucked up; I don't even want to deal with my shit. If you can just give me some time to work some things out, but at the same time be my friend again, I would really appreciate it. You can't ask me about what happened yet. Can you do that, Mols?" I beg her.

Molly looks down and then back up at me. Tears run down her face along with her mascara. "Yeah, Jay, I can do that. I've missed you." I grab her and hug her hard.

"Okay no more crying. I want you to tell me everything I've missed with you and Reed." She pulls back and finally smiles.

We sit outside for hours, and she tells me about how she and Reed finally "hooked up". Not a shocker there. She spoke of her and Reed's future plans, and how they were worried about being separated by their choice of colleges. The night air turns chilly, and I continue to listen. She did as I asked and didn't ask me about that night or the following month.

"So are you seeing anyone? Everyone is guessing that your new boyfriend is the one that beat up JT."

I didn't want to talk about that either, but I had to give her something.

"Ugh, that was a total misunderstanding. He's really an incredible guy." She smiles and knocks my knee with hers.

"Go on, what does this guy look like, and do I know him?" I laugh. I intend to tell her what a hottie he is when I remember that I totally blew him off this evening.

Jumping up, I look down at her. "Shit, I just remembered I stood him up." I run inside and grab my phone off the kitchen counter. It is almost ten o'clock at night and I had several text messages from him.

Kane – I'll meet u outside the gym
Kane – R U coming???

Molly must have followed me inside the house. "Is he mad at you?"

"I really don't know. It's crazy Molly because I've only known him for about a week now, but it feels like so much longer. We have this crazy connection, and when I'm with him, for the first time in years I feel whole. The only problem is that since he came into my life, everything I've built around me is falling apart. He's working two jobs and trying to build a company with his brother. He barely has time for me, much less my emotional complications."

I hear the roar of a motorcycle outside the window and know instantly who it is. "Well I guess you are going to meet him." In that instant, I realize how red and swollen Molly's eyes are and knew mine matched hers. "I'm guessing my face looks as red as yours?" I ask her.

She laughs and says, "Best friends always tell each other the truth and girl, you look a hot mess." I actually giggle with her. The doorbell chimes, and our laughter grows louder.

She follows me to the front door. I hear her gasp behind me when she finally sees him through the window.

"Holy hell, Jay. That is one fine man."

I could only nod in agreement. When I open the door, I notice first off he must have come straight from the gym. He has on a ragged t-shirt and baggy gym shorts with black tennis shoes. His eyes go from anger to concern when he sees my face.

"Did something happen, Jay?" He grabs me through the door and pulls me towards him. Crushing me in a hug, I feel his body tighten and realize he finally sees Molly behind me. I pull away and introduce them.

"Kane, this is my best friend Molly." I look at Molly as she nods at me. She looks at him and brings her hand up in a little wave.

"Nice to meet you, Kane. Sorry to run, but I've got to get home." She steps around us and turns back to me. "I will meet you at your car in the morning. Okay?" I nod in agreement, and then she says what we always used to say when leaving each other, "Great. Love you. Bye."

"Love you. Bye." I say back.

Kane pulls me through the door and closes it behind him. He looks at the dark foyer and house. He narrows his eyes at me. "Are your parents ever home with you?" I had already told him my parents traveled with their jobs.

"Not really." I am normally glad to be alone.

"You stood me up tonight. Is this going to be a continuing thing with us? You know, me always wondering if you're going to show up or not."

"I am so sorry, Molly came over to talk, and to be honest, it's been awhile for us. Before I knew it, time had flown by, and I just forgot."

He looks at me and says, "Next time just text me. I couldn't concentrate tonight, and all my sparring partners kicked my ass. Then instead of riding home, I came straight here. Sweaty as shit and all."

He looks great to me. I step up to kiss him, and at the same time my stomach lets out a loud growl. We both laugh.

"Hungry?" He asks. I nod and smile up at him. "So am I. I was hoping to take you out for a late dinner after the gym."

I look at him and ask, "Why don't I fix us something to eat? How does an omelet sound?"

"Sounds great to me. Do you care if I grab my stuff and take a shower first?"

I like the thought of him using my shower. "Sure. Go grab your stuff, and I'll start cooking."

He runs outside to grab his bag and then follows me to my room. I notice him looking around, but he says nothing. My room is very girly with a pink and white shabby chic theme. I grab a towel for him and leave the room. He doesn't try to stop me, but part of me wishes he would ask me to join.

By the time he comes back down stairs, I have our omelets ready at the bar. He had changed into a soft pair of blue jeans, plain blue shirt, and was now barefoot. He sits down, and I can't help staring at him. He cocks his eye at me and smiles.

"Like what you see?"

I hand him a bottle of water as I nod my head. "Yeah, I guess I do."

He grabs his fork and begins eating. "This is really good, Jay."

"Thanks. My dad used to make the best omelets, so I guess I learned from him."

We talk more about my parents and then more about his mom. He really wants to move her down here to be with him and Cole, but he wants to start building her a house first. God, I really love a man who loves his mother.

"So when are your parents coming home?"

I am sitting here trying not to think about how yummy he looks when he asks that question. Is he asking so he could stay with me tonight?

"A couple of days." I swallow hard. He doesn't say anything, and we both finish our food.

He stands and grabs our plates, rinsing them, and loading them into the dishwasher. I say nothing and just continue to stare at him. He turns my way and comes to stand right in front of me.

"I'm really tired, Jay. Really tired, but not tired enough for you." He leans down and gently kisses my lips. "Something tells me that this is not the right time for us yet, but I really want to hold you. I've got to get a decent night of sleep, and I haven't done that since I met you."

I bring my hand up and run it over his buzzed hair. It tickles my hand, and he closes his eyes.

"Okay, if you can be superman, and refrain from touching me, I can be your superwoman."

He laughs at my choice of words. "Girl, I think you are more like my glowing green rock, but I'm going to try. Let's go to bed. I am dead tired."

I reach for his hand and let him lead me back upstairs to my room.

"I'm going to take a quick shower, and I'll meet you in bed." I notice him swallow hard and grin. This isn't going to be as easy as he thought it would be.

"Sure," he says, "but hurry up, I like to snuggle."

I groan walking into my bathroom and shut the door. This is going to be a long night.

I think I broke the record for the fastest shower ever. One part of me worried that he would come and join me, and the other worried when he didn't. I did want to just sleep with him, but now I want more. I brush my wet hair out and rub coconut lotion all over my body. We would just have to see how he acts when I join him in bed.

When I step back into my room, I hear the soft sound of snoring and laugh. He really was tired, and he had fallen asleep sitting up against the headboard. His chest is bare, and the cover is pulled to his waist. I wonder if he has on boxers or briefs. I tip-toe to my side of the bed, pull the covers back, and climb in.

God he is so beautiful. I just want to stare at him. I want to rub my hands all over his chest and kiss every little scar I can see. Pulling the covers back, I glance underneath. Darn, he wears briefs. Smiling, I gently wake him. "Lay down with me." He never opens his eyes as he turns toward me and scoots down in the bed. I turn my back to his chest, and he pulls me closer, spooning his body to mine. I didn't think I could fall asleep like this, but before I know it, I am out.

I am in the school gym in one of the back closets. We keep paint here for the cheerleaders to make spirit signs for school. Everyone had left after practice, but I am meeting Molly and Reed for dinner, so I need to waste some time. I thought I would make some posters for the upcoming first game. We are sophomores, and JT is going to be starting as quarterback. I am so proud of him. The closet is actually large enough that I can sit down and paint.

I hear a knock at the door and look up to see him standing there. "Hey." I smile up at him. Molly was right, he does have pretty eyes. "What are you still doing here?" I ask him as he walks into the closet, closes the door, and locks it. Later, I would realize that I didn't even question him locking the door. He squats down next time, raises his hand, and brushes the hair out of my eyes. I jerk back. He has touched me before, but it was always brief grazes against my arm in the hallways. Nothing improper, just little brushes here and there. Didn't he do that with everyone?

"James, you don't have to pretend with me anymore. I know what you want, and we don't have to tell JT."

What is he talking about? His eyes don't look friendly anymore.

In fact, they look hard, and something evil gleams in them. Want? Need? Lust? Hate? I try to jump up, but in less than a second, he lunges and has my arms pinned above my body in one hand. I am flat against the floor. His other hand covers my mouth, and his body lays heavy on top of mine.

"Shut up, James, nobody is going to hear you. It's just you in me in the gym. The entire football team is on the field practicing, and everyone else is gone. You knew this was coming. I'm just going to get a little taste of what you give JT all the time. Just a little taste."

His breathing becomes heavy. "I'm going to move my hand, and if you scream, I'm going to hit you. If someone finds out about us, they're not going to believe you, Jay. They're going to believe me. Everyone can see how you flaunt your shit all around school. You are such a fucking cock tease." He moves his hand away from my mouth, and I am too paralyzed with fear to say anything or move. He flips my t-shirt above my chest so it covers my face, and he leaves it there. He undoes my bra clasp and bites down on my nipple roughly. I cry out in pain.

"Shut the fuck up, and don't make a sound."

He repeats the action on other nipple, and I bite my lip to hold back the cries. He pulls my shorts and panties down.

"Sweet Jesus, Jay. I bet you make JT want to come every time he looks at your naked little body." He moves my arms down to either side of me.

Suddenly, the fight and flight instinct takes over, and I try to fight him off. I raise my arms and start hitting him, trying to buck his body off mine. He squeezes my arms harshly and starts to shake my body against the floor. My head snaps back on the concrete, and pain radiates through my body. My vision wavers and the shirt over my face falls down. His face is twisted, not in pain, but in a sick pleasure. He is loving this.

"Fight me. I want you to." My body feels heavy, and I am so tired. My stomach starts to turn. I can feel vomit rise in the back of

my throat. His hands roam lower, grabbing my legs and squeezing hard. He leans back and pulls his shorts down. Then moving forward, he covers my body. One quick thrust into me, and I scream from the pain. "Shit," he says looking down at me and laughing as he covers my mouth with his hand. "I guess JT wasn't getting it after all." He begins moving, and the pain is unbearable. My vision blurs, and I let the darkness take me away.

Hands shake my body, bringing me awake. "Wake up, Jay. It's okay baby, I'm here." Kane's voice whispers over my soft cries. My face is buried in his chest as he kisses the top of my head, and his hand strokes my back, comforting me. I snuggle closer and let myself be carried back to sleep, feeling safe.

chapter Six

The sun streams through my bedroom windows, softy lighting his face as he lay next to me. His features are strong, but in the soft light, they are so beautiful. We are facing each other, and his hands are wrapped around my waist. Kane sleeps so peacefully, and that peace spreads to me. I haven't felt this way in a long time.

I lean forward and lightly kiss the tip of his nose. The sides of his mouth lift upward into a smile, and his eyes flutter open, their green orbs still sleepy from his slumber.

"Hi," he whispers.

"Hi back." I say and grin. We stare at each other for minutes.

Finally, he raises his hand from my waist, and his finger outlines my face. I close my eyes just enjoying the moment. My mind goes back to last night, and I realize that he's the first to hold me after a nightmare. Normally, when I have that particular dream, I don't go back to sleep. My mind refuses to shut down. It plays over and over in my head. Last night, when he held me, I was able to return to sleep in his arms. I was safe, loved, and maybe even cherished.

With my eyes still closed, I feel his lips follow the same outline his finger traced. A tear squeezes out of my left eye and glides down my cheek. His lips capture it and drink it away.

"Please, don't cry," he begs. I open my eyes and look into his concerned ones.

"It's a happy tear," my voice chokes back. He brings his lips back to mine, and our gazes lock as he kisses me. He pulls back first.

"I can wait for you, Jay. My body hurts for yours, but I'll wait for you." I move towards his lips again, wanting him to know that I'm ready for him. I am ready for us. Against my mouth he whispers, "Not yet. You're getting there. I want you mind, body, and soul. Do you understand what I am saying, Jay?"

Staring into his eyes, I do understand. What is between us is more than just now, and it scares me to death. I pull back.

"I guess I need to get dressed for school." Sitting up, I don't answer his question. He will not pressure me, and I know this. Walking into my bathroom, I begin to brush my teeth. Within minutes, he is standing next to me reaching for my toothbrush. He rinses it and applies more toothpaste. I watch as he brushes his teeth, staring at his reflection in the mirror the entire time. He finally rinses his mouth and turns to me.

"Do you want me to come back tonight and stay?" The question catches me off guard for a minute.

"Do you want to?" I ask, realizing that I do want him to come back.

He looks at me and nods his head. "Yes, I want to sleep next to you. Plus, I hate the idea that you are here alone." I smile at him. "Okay, my turn to cook you dinner tonight," he says as he leans in, kissing my cheek and smiling back at me. "See you tonight, babe," he says and walks away.

I think of that smile as I dress and leave for school. Kane wants more from me than just my body or one night. The strangest part for me is that I want to give it to him. He makes me want a future. He makes me want to let the past go, but how am I supposed to do that when everyone suddenly wants the truth? I hate the saying, "The truth can set you free". The truth can't set me free. It can fuck my future fifty ways to Sunday. In my mind, the horror has already happened, and no one can take it back. Having the whole school, my friends, and family know will only make everything worse.

I park my car and get out. I see Molly and Reed walking towards me with Molly practically dragging him behind her. She is grinning from ear to ear, but Reed looks leery of me. Can't really say I blame him.

As Molly finally approaches me, she lets go of him, grabs me around my neck, and hugs me. I look up and then smile at Reed.

"I guess hell finally froze over, huh?" He asks while wrapping his arms around Molly and me. We all laugh. Moments later, when we finally all pull back, Molly smiles at me as she reaches for Reed's hand.

"I told Reed about our talk last night. We want things the way they were." Molly says.

Reed looks at me and says, "We've missed you, Jay. I agree that we just go forward from here and enjoy our senior year together."

"That works for me. I love you guys, and I've really missed you." I lean forward and kiss both of their cheeks. We link arms and head into school talking about nothing important, but suddenly it means everything to me.

I finally make it to first period, and Cal is sending me that big grin of his. "What are you smiling at?" I can't help but ask and smile back at him.

"Looks like someone is finally removing that gigantic stick out of her ass and moving on," he answers. I know he's being funny, and I roll my eyes at him. Of course, he had to ruin the moment. He continues, "Have you thought about coming out to support JT on Friday?" I shake my head him and turn away.

The day races by. I sit with Molly and Reed during lunch, and it is like the last two years never happened. They didn't push for answers, and we didn't talk about JT. We talk about their relationship, the future, and, of course, Molly wants to know every-thing about Kane. I think I smile and laugh more today than I have in years.

Reed notices Rhye staring at me during lunch. "Ok Jay, I have to ask this. What the hell is up with you and Rhye? Dude is staring you up like you are his last supper. I've noticed him doing this for a while. What gives?"

My eyes follow Reed's to see Rhye sitting across the lunch-room, watching me. When he knows he has my attention, he stands and nods his head then walks out the door. I turn back to Reed and Molly.

"Just a mess I created for myself. I don't think he's used to a girl not falling all over him." Neither one of them have anything to say to that.

At the end of the day, the final bell rings, and I meet up again with Molly and Reed to walk out to the parking lot.

"Just like old times," Molly says and smiles at me. "Do you want to go have pizza with Reed and me tonight?"

"I really would, Mols, but Kane is cooking dinner for me." I can't keep the grin off my face, and she laughs.

"Ah, young love. I can forgive you for that. How about tomorrow we go downtown dancing? Reed and I haven't been out to a club in forever, and you can bring Mr. McHottie with you."

Laughing back at her, I say, "I'll ask him, but either way it's a date."

When we get to my car, Molly notices before I do what's waiting for me on my windshield. I see the slip of white paper and this time, a single red flower is with it. My stomach instantly turns, and I feel the blood leave my face. My body freezes.

"Ooh, someone has a love note." I watch as Molly grabs the paper and opens it before I can say or do anything.

Glancing at Reed, I notice that he is watching me. His eyes grow as he sees the panic in mine. I finally try to grab the note but not before she reads it. I hear her gasp.

"What the hell is this, Jay?" Molly looks upset, and Reed tries to grab the note, but I am able to jerk it from Molly's grasp.

Opening to read it, my body shakes with fury.

I think it's about time for round two. I can't wait to take that tight little body again. I'm coming for you. Will you fight me again or just let me have it this time?

Reed jerks the paper from my hands to read it. I'm too ashamed and mad to say anything.

"What is this, Jay?" He yells at me and continues, "How long has Rhye been bothering you with this shit?" My head turns toward his. "How long as he been stalking you and leaving these notes?" I guess he notices the surprise look on my face. His voice lowers, and he asks, "Are they even from him or someone else?"

Grabbing the note back, I look at both of them and shove it in my front pocket.

"It's just his sick and twisted way of getting to me. It just threw me for a second." I smile the biggest fake smile I can. "He's an asshole. We send these stupid notes back and forth. It's just a twisted game between us."

Reed looks right at me, and he sounds so sad. "When did rape become a joke?"

I gasp and stutter, "Th-that's not it. It wasn't like that, Reed. Just don't read anything into this, okay? Please?" My voice begs him and so do my eyes. Looking at Molly, I could see the pity in her eyes and she shakes her head at me. "I've got to go guys. I'll see you both tomorrow."

Not waiting for either of them to respond, I jump in my car and start to pull away. I only glance up once to look into the rear view mirror. I see Molly lean into Reed for a hug, and he is watching my car drive away. They finally fade from my view. Isn't that what I always do? I run away from everyone and everything. The moment I think everything is getting easier, I realize this shit is never going to end.

I drive to the lake. There is this spot that JT would always take me to so we could just sit and talk. It's a wooded area that has a gentle slope to the water. I back my car up so I can face the water while sitting on the trunk. It is so quiet and peaceful here.

What is the point to all this pain? I have to either feel it or deal with it, and it's hurt too many people that I love. It's hurt me. The notes are because he wants me to hurt. He really gets off on that. I didn't turn him in, and it gave him power over me. Doesn't he know that I will end it all before I tell anyone?

Two weeks ago, I could have told you just how and where I would end this life. My life didn't mean anything to me. The only thing that mattered was the control that I had over it. I swore when I lost that again, it would be time. I pretty much cut all ties to those I love so that my death wouldn't hurt that much, and now look what I have done? I've ruined all that. In these past couple of weeks, I've mended those ties and made new ones.

My phone chirps alerting me to a text message. I pull it out of my pocket and see that it's from Kane.

Kane – how was school? working late tonight but will try to be at your house by 9...late dinner okay?

I place the phone beside me. What am I doing? Could I hurt this guy? Would I want to see his beautiful eyes dim toward me if he were to learn my secrets? I look back over the water, and that's when I hear a car pulling in behind me. I turn and notice immediately that it's JT's red truck. He should be at football practice. What is he doing here? He jumps out and marches right up to me. His face is red, and the rage pours off of him.

"Why aren't you at football practice?" I ask trying to deflect his anger.

"Fuck football practice. What did that motherfucker Rhye do? Don't you lie to me again, Jay. I swear, I will beat you to within an inch of your life if you do, and then you'll have a valid reason to be scared of me," he yells in my face.

JT is furious, and his jaw tightens as he grinds his teeth together. I know that I need to calm him down. Placing both of my hands on his shoulders, I calmly say to him, "Calm down, JT. I'll talk to you, but you have to calm down." He looks at my hands and then back at me. He takes a deep breath.

"Reed told me about the note. I was watching you all day. God, you, Molly, and Reed talking again just gave me hope for me and you. I watched what happened in the parking lot. After you left, I cornered Reed and made him tell me why you all looked upset. He told me about the note and flower on your car. Molly said she only grabbed it off your windshield and read it because she thought your new boyfriend had left it for you, but Reed said it wasn't from him. He thinks that Rhye left it. Is that who forced you, Jay? Was he the one that took you away from me?"

I gasp. "It wasn't like that with Rhye." JT narrows his eyes at me, and I continue, "He didn't force me, JT, and he wasn't my first." I knew I had to give him something, and that was as close to the truth as I could get for now. He backs away from me and turns around. He stands there silently, staring out over the water.

"So what, you like it rough then? Does it get you off that someone has to take it? Is that what I'm missing?" His voice is low, and he still faces away from me. His hands are gripping his waist tightly. JT's next question is hidden in a mumble, but I still hear it. "I was supposed to be your first, Jay. Why wasn't I your first?"

Jumping from the car, I walk to stand behind him. A love so intense fills me. I still loved this boy that stood in front of me. For the life of me, I wish I didn't, but I do. I place my hand on the middle of his back and whisper to him, "I was saving me for you." His body starts shaking with emotion, and he tries to turn around, but I don't let him. "No don't turn around. I just want you to listen to me, and I don't want you to look at me." I stroke his hard muscular back, shoulder to shoulder, as he lowers his chin to his chest.

"I know you've guessed what happened. I'm not going to lie to you anymore and say it didn't. God knows JT, I've lied to everyone, and I have my reasons. If I could go back and change time, I would, but I can't. I've begged you to move on. You have to or you will destroy me and you both. I can't talk about it. I can only beg you to let it go. Please dear Lord, just let it go."

His breathing halts, I can feel it from my hands on his back.

"Why didn't you tell me? Why, Jay?"

Clearing my voice, I continue to rub his back, not sure if I am comforting him or myself. My body is warming, and I am standing so close to him that I can see the hairs on the back of his neck stand up.

"I was ruined for you, JT. I wanted to come to you whole. I was ashamed, and then things just continued to get worse. The longer I ignored you, the easier to break away it became, but I never stopped loving you. I can't stop loving you." My voice whispers to him.

He suddenly turns around, but he doesn't touch me. We stand almost nose to nose. Looking into those clear blue eyes, I know I will always love him. He will hold a huge part of my heart, forever and always.

"You still love me," he states. It wasn't a question, and I know he sees the answer in my eyes. He slowly brings his hand up and rubs the tips of his fingers across my lips. Closing my eyes, I feel his lips on mine. Lightly, he kisses me, but he keeps his arms at his side. He speaks in between kisses, "I love you, Jay. I've always loved only you. Please, just love me."

His words rip me apart. How much damage had I caused this beautiful boy? I owe him this, and I want to give him a little part of me, just enough to heal him. I can't even begin to think about what it will cost me.

Reaching for his face, I cradle his cheeks in my hands. The bruises are a faded green color now. My mouth finds his, and I kiss him. He groans, but he doesn't reach for me. Years fall away, and I remember with a vengeance how much he was a part of my life. Sucking on his tongue, he finally grabs my hips, but he doesn't pull me toward him. Instead he pushes me away. My breaths are coming in pants and so are his.

"That is the second hardest thing I've ever done," he states between breaths. "I have to be sure, Jay. Are you choosing me over him? Is that what this is?"

I know he means Kane. His eyes plead with me to answer his questions with a "yes." I want to, but I am confused. Turning around, I walk toward the shoreline. The sun is mirrored on the water, and it gleams gold. He comes to stand behind me.

"Do you know what I miss more than anything?" He speaks softly behind my ear. "I miss that you were my best friend, and we told each other everything. It didn't matter how corny or stupid it was. You always listened, and you never laughed. We would come out here and just talk for hours. When you walked away, I had no one to talk to. No one, Jay." He pauses, and I don't know what to say. The silence is killing me.

"I love you, JT, but I think I love him too. This is such a mess, and I didn't plan this. I, honest to God, thought I was over you and I am just now realizing I never was."

Lifting my hands, I cover my eyes. He steps up behind me and pulls my back against his chest. He wraps his arms around me, and I lean back against him. He kisses the top of my head and lowers his mouth to my ear.

"I have one question for you. Can you give me just as much of a chance to be with you as you give him? I don't want to say that you owe me that, but if I have to fight dirty for you, I just might. Please Jay, I'm asking that you just give us the chance that we should have had in the first place."

How could I not give him this chance? I had to do it, and maybe it would give both of us the closure we needed. Nodding my head "yes", I turn towards him.

"I have to be honest with Kane and tell him."

JT nods his head as he leans down to kiss me. His kiss is gentle, and I lean back.

"I can wait. Honestly, Jay, I was planning on waiting forever for you."

Smiling up at him, I return, "You were, huh?" He smiles back at me.

"I'll take you anyway I can get you, Jay."

Our conversation is broken by the ringing of his cell phone. I think it had been ringing for a while, but it fell to the wayside.

"JT, you need to get that." He groans to let go of me and reaches for his phone.

"Shit," he says as he glances down and reads his text message. "Jay, I've got to get back to practice. Coach is threatening to bench me for the first game if I don't go back now. Can I come by your house tonight?"

"Kane is coming over. I need to talk with him." I can tell he is pissed, but he tries to hide it.

"Well just promise me this. Don't be with him, okay? If you are really going to give us a chance, can you please just promise me that?"

Looking at him, I decide that a little more honesty would help. "We haven't had sex yet, if that's what you're asking." His eyes fill with relief, and I finish, "I promise that until we decide about us, I will not cross that line, but I don't want to use either of you, and I'm not going to lie, I do have strong feelings for him."

He kisses me fast and pulls back. "I just want one more chance with you. Like I said, I'll take it any way I can get it. The only thing I ask, Jay, is that you're honest with me." He kisses me once more and says, "I'll text you later." Walking toward his truck, he looks back once more before getting in and driving away.

What did I just do? I lean against my car and shake my head. What am I going to tell Kane? I have really strong feelings for him, and I don't want to let him go, but I love JT. I have to talk with Kane. Damn, I forgot he texted me earlier.

Me – *That's fine…See you tonight…*

I would talk with him tonight, but damn if I know what I will say.

chapter Seven

It is dark as I pull my car into my driveway. I had driven around for a while after I left the lake with no set destination. I did stop by the deli on the way home to get some sandwiches for Kane. I texted him while I was there to let him know I had dinner covered. Bringing everything into the house, I went ahead and laid out the food on the kitchen counter. It is close to nine o'clock, and Kane should be here shortly. My phone vibrates in my pocket.

JT – I love you Jay.

Closing my eyes, I take a deep breath. What have I done, and what am I going to say to Kane? My thoughts are interrupted by his voice. I had left the front door unlocked for him.

"Jay, where are you?"

"I'm in the kitchen," I answer. He walks in smiling, and his clothes are dirty. His shirt and pants are covered in dust. Leaning in, he gives me a kiss and looks hungrily at the spread of food on the counter.

"Goodness, I'm starving, but I want a shower first. I'm going to run upstairs, and then I'll come down and eat with you, okay?"

"Yeah, that's fine." He kisses me again and turns to run upstairs.

Moving around the kitchen, I take out the plates. I open the fridge, grab him a beer, and sit it on the counter. He is back before I have everything ready.

"Thanks for getting dinner," he says as he reaches for me and kisses me so deeply that my knees go weak. He pulls himself away and looks me in the eyes. "What's wrong, Jay? I can tell something is bothering you."

I push him away and shake my head. "Let's just eat. What else can I get you?"

"Stop, Jay."

I look up at him.

"First, we are going to talk about whatever it is that is bothering you."

I sigh and sit down on the bar stool. "I had a talk with JT today." He looks at me, waiting for me to continue. "Things are just so complicated with us. He wants me to give him another chance." Kane leans back against the counter and crosses his arms and legs.

"Did you tell him that you had a boyfriend now?" His eyes never leave mine.

I lift my eyebrows and ask, "I have a boyfriend?"

"Fuck yeah, you have a boyfriend. Damn Jay, did you not listen to me this morning?"

"I think I would have remembered if you had said you were my boyfriend. In fact, the only thing I've heard clearly is that you don't want anything serious."

He leans up and uncrosses his legs and arms. "I didn't want anything serious, but I keep ending up back here with you. Seems to me that question was already answered. So what did you tell him?"

I close my eyes and whisper, "I told him that I thought I might be in love with you." Looking up, I see Kane's eye grow warm, but they snap shut when I finish, "but I also told him that I just realized today that I am still in love with him too."

His voice is low when he asks his next question, "Who do you want to be with, Jay? That's what I want to know."

"I don't know, Kane. We've just met, but part of me feels like I've known you forever, and I do have deep feelings for you. You have to understand, there were things that happened that pulled JT and I apart. There was never any closure for us, and we need that. I owe that to him."

"You don't owe him anything. Just answer me, Jay. Me or him? It's one or the other, because it sure as hell, isn't both." His eyes are hard, and he is pissed.

"I want you Kane, but I promised to give him a chance." I reach to grab his arm, but he pulls away from me.

"That's not how it works, Jay. You can't be with me while you decide if you want to be with him." He shakes his head, walks out of the kitchen, and goes up the stairs. I follow him.

"Kane, you don't understand. Please just stop and listen to me." I walk behind him into my bedroom, where he must have unpacked an overnight bag earlier. He begins packing everything back up. Grabbing his shaving kit before he can touch it, I hold it away from him. "Please just give me five seconds."

He stands with his hands on his hips and asks, "Him or me, Jay? Tell me now." I start to panic because I know he will walk out forever, and I don't want to lose him.

"You, Kane. It's you that I need to be with." Reaching for him, I try to kiss his mouth, but he turns his face from me.

"You need to be with me, Jay, or do you want to be with me? Which is it? Because to me it makes a difference. I've come to care so much for you in such a short period of time, more than anyone else before you. I don't want to get hurt Jay, and just so we are clear, you can hurt me."

I look deep into his eyes and say what is in my heart. "I said 'need' because with every fiber of my being, I feel that you and I are meant to be together. That all this pain and fear that I have experienced would be worth it for just one moment with you. If you want me to say that I want to be with you, than that's true also. I want you so bad that my mind and body crave you. Just one look or one word from you, and my body goes up in flames. I want you Kane, and I desperately need you."

Kane reaches for me and kisses me hard. His mouth devours

mine, and we both start trying to undress each other as the fire rages higher. I push his shirt up and off as he tries to unbutton mine. He finally gives up and rips it open. Buttons jump everywhere as they land on the floor, but his lips never leave mine. My hands go to his shorts, and I tug them down as he steps out of them. Staring into my eyes the entire time, he finally pulls his mouth from mine. He unsnaps my shorts, and they drift down my legs. I am left in nothing but bra and panties, and he stands only in his briefs.

"Jay," my name comes out like a prayer. "Be mine. Be only mine," he whispers to me.

"Yes, Kane, only yours," I answer, and his eyes close. He leans in and kisses me gently, clasping both of my hands at my side. His soft lips move across my eyes, and tears spring behind them. My hands ache to touch him, so I try and pull my hands free, but he keeps them interlocked in his. Finally, his eyes slowly open, and I see what is shining so brightly within them.

"I love you too," the words leave me.

He groans and finally releases my hands so he can pick me up. I wrap my legs tightly around his waist, and one of my arms wraps around his neck while the opposite hand runs across his shaved head. He carries me to the bed and lies down on top of me. Unhooking my bra, he pulls it away, and his breathing becomes heavy. Kissing down my neck to my chest, he slips his hand under the edge of my panties and starts to drag them down. Suddenly, he moves his hand and mouth away from me as I try to pull him back.

"Please, don't stop, Kane," I beg him.

"Listen Jay, someone is ringing your door bell like crazy." I am so lost in us that it takes a minute to hear what he is saying.

"I don't care, Kane. Please don't stop." I can tell he is warring with himself.

"We have to make sure it's not important, and since this is your house, that means you have to go down there, but I'm going with you". He kisses my mouth softly one more time before he stands up and lifts me with him. Kane goes to my dresser and grabs a t-shirt and cotton shorts for me. Not saying a word, he puts the shirt on me without a bra and then helps me step into the shorts. He dresses himself quickly. When we are both ready, he grabs my hand, and we head downstairs.

"Quit pouting, Jay. It just makes me want you more." He smiles back at me and stops to kiss me.

I didn't see anybody standing in front of the door, but then all of a sudden, it dawns on me that it could be JT. How the hell could I forget about JT? I had promised him that I would not sleep with Kane, and that's what I almost did. What kind of person am I? Am I so broken that I can't keep one promise to the person that deserves it most? Kane stands behind me as I open the door.

Holding my breath, I know I'm going to see JT, but it isn't him sitting on my doorstep. It is Rhye, and he is drunk or high. He stands up swaying and laughing.

"What the fuck, Rhye?"

"I hear it's more like rape than fucking. Though the last time we were together, if I remember correctly, it was more of YOU raping ME."

Kane steps around me to see who it is. He looks at me and asks, "What does this fucker want?"

"Rapist," Rhye slurs out. "Evidently according to your girl here, that's what I am. Really Jay, why don't you just stab me in the heart? It's got to be better than hearing that you told people that I raped you. It was never like that with us. Why would you lie and tell anyone that I forced you?" His voice breaks as tears come to his eyes. "I fucking love you, Jay. Don't you know that?"

My jaw falls open. I knew that Rhye wanted to have sex with me, but I really didn't think he cared about me, much less loved me. He seems to sober up a little as he stares at me.

"What, Jay? You didn't think I had any feelings? Forget you. Yeah, I messed up and slept with that groupie. Jay, I only did it because when you were with me, the whole time I knew you wished it was JT. The night before I slept with her, you called out his name when you were with me. That killed me, Jay. I was already half in love with you then."

Kane stiffened next to me, so I quickly ask, "How did you get here, Rhye? You didn't drive yourself did you?"

"Why do you care, Jay? You've been on a one way road to self-destruct since you broke up with JT. Everyone knows it." He looks over me to Kane. "Ever ask about her future? She doesn't have one planned. You want to know why? She doesn't plan on being here." He laughs and looks at me. "What, you thought that was a secret, Jay? I bet you've already have it all planned out."

Visibly, I blanch at his words. My mouth goes dry, and my stomach churns. I turn toward Kane, and he goes from watching Rhye to watching me.

"What's he talking about, Jay? Why don't you plan on being here? Where do you plan on going?" I watch the different scenarios run across his face until he reaches the one he knows is true.. Before he can say anything, I turn back towards Rhye.

My hand reaches out and slaps him hard across the face. I don't know who is more surprised, me, Rhye, or Kane. Rhye grabs his cheek and looks at me. His face goes white as a ghost.

"Shit Jay. I'm sorry. JT came down to the bar wanting to kick my ass, and we started to fight. Of course the band pulled us apart, and he said why he is pissed. It just hurt to hear what you had said. He left, so I got hammered, and Chris drove me here."

"So you have a ride home. Good. Then get off my doorstep. Don't ever talk to me again, Rhye. I apologize for what JT said, but I told him that you didn't rape me. I told him that what happened between you and me was consensual. I'll make sure to set anyone else straight on that matter, but stay away from me."

I step back into the house, grabbing Kane as I go. He allows me to pull him in, and I shut the door. Walking away from him, I turn to go into the kitchen. All the food is still on the counter where I had left it. Picking up a sandwich and a pickle, I put them on a plate and sit down at the bar. Kane walks in and grabs the other stool beside me.

We sit in silence, not looking at each other. Kane places his clasped hands on top of the counter. He starts to speak but then shakes his head and doesn't say anything. I push the food around on my plate, not realizing that silent tears are falling down my face. Feeling ashamed, I can't even look at Kane. We both continue to sit there, ignoring each other. Finally, he reaches for my hand. I look up into his face and unshed tears stare back at me.

"I had the tattoo put on my neck to remind me to always be true to myself. Not to let others bring me down and to live my life, my way. Shit happens in life, Jay. You can let it destroy you, or you can fight back and live life to the fullest," he pauses and takes a deep breath. "Believe it or not, my freshman year in high school, I was a scrawny little shit. My best friend Matt and I took a lot of crap from upper classman, picking on both of us because of our size. We hadn't hit our growth spurts yet, and Matt never would, because he got tired of the bullies at our school, and one night, he fatally shot himself."

His voice breaks, but he continues, "It killed me. My best friend since we were kids ended his life, leaving me alone. I can tell you, Jay, nothing that happens in this life is worth killing yourself over. Time passes, and you can decide to change your future. You don't let what some assholes say or do, direct you. In this life, it only matters what you do with it."

Kane stands up and pulls me into his arms. He picks me up, cradling me to his chest, and I wrap my arms around his neck. Slowly, he carries me upstairs to my bedroom and lays me on my bed. He slides next to me and wraps me in his arms. Holding me tight, the exhaustion envelops me, and I close my eyes to fall into a deep sleep.

My hand shields the bright light from my eyes. When it finally dims, I look around me to see that I'm standing back inside the white room. I'm alone, and I look around for a way out, but there are no doors. I close my eyes tightly, and I feel him behind me. Slipping his arms around my waist, he presses his body close to mine and speaks into my ear. "No one will love you but me when they find out what you've done. They will all blame you and call you a whore. A murderer. You're losing control, James. Are you ready to join me yet?"

He holds his hand out, and I look down into his palm. Multi-colored pills fill it. He brings them to my mouth, but I turn my head away and he laughs. His voice whispers, "I can wait."

Chapter Eight

The sound of my phone vibrating wakes me from sleep in the morning. Turning over, I see that Kane is not beside me. I grab my phone to read my new text message.

Kane – Need to get to work early. Didn't want to wake you. We'll talk later.

Not wanting to think about last night, I get up and dress quickly for school, throwing on some skinny jeans and a shirt. I can't imagine what Kane thinks about me. My mind refuses to go there. It's too much, happening way too fast, and it's screaming at me. Running downstairs, I grab my book bag and head out the door.

Molly is waiting by herself in the parking lot when I get to school. She smiles at me as I step out of my car.

"I'm a shit." She says and continues, "I shouldn't have read your note. It wasn't any of my business, and I'm sorry."

"I'm sorry too, Mols, but I need you to know that that note wasn't from Rhye. I'm sorry if I mislead you or Reed into thinking that was who wrote it." I can tell she is confused. The look on her face says it all. "Listen, I've got way bigger problems this morning, and I may need your help."

"What is it, Jay? You know I am here for you."

Looking into her eyes, I see that statement to be true. "Okay, just hear me out, and then help me figure out what I am going to do."

98

I tell her about the conversation between JT and me along with everything that happened last night with Kane and Rhye. When I finally finish, she looks at me and places her head in her hands.

"This is all, my fault. I shouldn't have reacted like that yesterday, and damn Reed for saying anything to JT."

"Mols, it's okay. I just have to figure out what I am going to do about all of them."

"Who do you want to be with?"

"See, that's the problem. I thought I was over JT, and now I know I'm not, but I'm also in love with Kane. He makes me feel safe, and he doesn't represent anything from my past like JT does. When I look at JT, I think about what we used to have, but when I see Kane, I know what I want now. I feel like I owe JT a chance for us, but Kane says I don't. I'm just so confused."

"Jay, you can't do this to JT. He will not survive losing you again. I can tell you really care about Kane, and trust me girl, I've seen him and know why you feel that way. Part of me feels that if you think there is any chance for you and JT, then you owe him that. I'm sorry, but that's how I feel. He loves you so much, Jay. Think about what you have put him through?"

I know what she is saying. I hear someone call my name, and I look up. Walking towards me is the reason I am feeling so conflicted. JT has on a pair of faded jeans and a t-shirt with the school logo on it. He also has the biggest smile I have ever seen.

Molly pats my arm and says, "Think of that little boy from kindergarten that told you he was going to marry you one day and always stayed true to that." She walks away, smiling at JT.

"I'm not sure what to do, Jay? My arms ache to pull you to me right now. I want to kiss you in front of everyone and claim you, but I'm kind of lost as to what you want me to do." He stops in front of me and crosses his arms against his chest.

"We take it slow, one day at a time. No fighting, and yeah I know about you and Rhye. He came to the house last night. Don't ask me about Kane, and I will not talk to him about you." I still need time to figure out what I am going to do, but Molly is right. I can't keep hurting JT, and telling him that I am going to be with Kane, would kill him.

"Alright Jay, we'll play this your way. Can I walk you to class?"

"Lead the way," I say to him and smile.

He wraps his arm around my shoulders, and we walk towards the school. I see the surprised looks as we pass students and teachers. A group of young freshman girls actually giggle and stare as we walk by.

JT laughs and turns his face towards mine. "Can you imagine all the gossip by lunch time?"

"Ugh, I don't want to think about it. The rumor mill will probably have me pregnant with your baby."

"I'll confirm that the twins are due in the spring," he jokes and kisses my cheek.

"Well, you better get that football scholarship so you can make it to the big time to support us." I nudge his ribs with my elbow.

We arrive at my first period class, and Cal just happens to be at the door. He smiles when he sees us together.

"What do we have here? It can't be my two favorite people actually getting along and not fighting? The world is surely coming to an end." He slaps JT playfully on the arm. "Coach wants us to meet with him next period."

"I'll be there," JT replies and turns away from Cal toward me. "See you at lunch?"

"Sure," I say as I turn away and head into class. Cal comes in after me and sits right by me. He's grinning from ear to ear. I can't help asking him, "Why are you smiling?"

"All is right in the world. What's not to be happy about?"

I shake my head. His happiness is infectious, but it doesn't last. Class starts, and my mind tunes out to think about what I am doing. I meant it last night when I told Kane that I wanted and needed him. At that moment, my mind and body belonged to him, but part of me longs for JT. In my heart, I know that I can't turn away from JT without finding out if we have a future, but what am I going to do about Kane? I'm worried about him leaving this morning without talking to me.

The bell rings, and class is dismissed. When I arrive in second period, Rhye is already in his seat. He looks up at me and then looks back down. I decide that we both need to cool off. My mind is still going over what he said to me last night. Even though he spoke the truth, I can't believe he said it out loud.

I think back to what Kane said to me about his friend. He had lost someone he cared about. I could see the pain and regret in his eyes that he still carries for Matt. Could I ever really put someone through that? Do I still feel the same way? So many thoughts go through my head, and for the rest of the morning, I just move on autopilot. I do not see JT or Molly until lunch.

When I walk into the cafeteria, Molly waves me over to her and Reed. He stands when I walk over and leans in to hug me, "Sorry, Jay."

"It's okay Reed," I say to him. I knew he was talking about the note and telling JT.

I sit on the other side of Molly, and before I can talk to her, my chair is pulled back.

JT leans over and kisses me on my lips in front of everyone. I'm too stunned to do anything but respond, which I automatically do. His kiss is familiar, and my body reacts to it. My arms go up and around his neck. There is definitely still something between us. I lose myself just a little to him.

The sound of clapping snaps me out of the passionate kiss. Stunned, I turn around and see that almost every single student in the cafeteria, including Molly and Reed, are standing there clapping and whistling. Cal is the loudest with his whooping and hollering. I even see Mrs. Davis smile as she walks by, pretending not to see. JT looks down at me and pulls me to standing. A laugh escapes me.

"Do you think we should give them an encore?" He asks, but he doesn't wait for my answer as he captures my mouth again.

This kiss is a tad sweeter and softer. I can't help but melt. This moment feels like it's supposed to happen.

He pulls back from me and whispers gently in my ear, "Please tell me you feel it, Jay. That this is where you and I should have been all along? Don't tell me it's just me."

"JT," I start to say, but words get stuck in my throat. I nod my head "yes" and hear him gasp. He grips me tighter and hugs me closer.

By now everyone has sat down to eat. We are still receiving glances, and Molly is beaming at me. Reed still looks pretty leery, and I still don't blame him. My feelings are all over the place. Can you be bipolar in love? That's how I feel. One part of me only loves Kane, but the other part has always been JT's.

JT sits down in my chair, pulling me onto his lap, and wraps his arms around my stomach. He won't stop looking at me, and I can feel my cheeks blushing.

"Quit staring at me," I tell him.

"Damn Jay, when did you grow up and become this beautiful woman? I'm sorry I kissed you in front of everyone, but I walk into the cafeteria, and there you are. I didn't see anyone else. You were just sitting there, and I needed to kiss you." He blushes and says, "My heart jumped when I saw you. That's how much you mean to me." I place my finger across his lips to halt his words.

"I know, JT. You're not the only one feeling it." He grips me closer to him and kisses the top of my head.

"Ok, you guys, I can't stand it anymore. Talk. I need some answers." Molly is almost bouncing off her seat with excitement.

Looking at JT, he smiles at me, and I turn to answer her. "We are taking it slowly. Very slowly," I repeat and glance at JT. He nods so he must be happy with my answer. "Are you going to get some food?"

"Jay, if you think for one second that I am getting up from this spot until I have to, you are crazy. I'm not letting you out of my lap until someone makes me. If that means I have to starve to death, it will be worth it." We all laugh, but I hug him a little tighter because it makes me happy that he feels that way about me.

"Mr. Higgins, I do believe Miss Stevenson can find her own seat. I don't believe she needs to share yours," Coach Branch vehemently says to JT as he stands over us. It surprises everyone at the table, and I try to jump up, but JT holds me still.

"C'mon, Coach B. You can't blame me for wanting to hold my girl for a second can you?" He tries to break the overwhelming tension.

"Don't make me ask again, JT. I would hate to have you benched for the first game. I'm sure that would not help your college prospects." Coach Branch glares at JT, and he stares back. The silence has become uncomfortable for everyone. I finally wiggle out of JT's arms.

"I'm going to grab something to drink," I say and walk away. When I get back with my soda, Coach Branch is gone, but JT, Molly and Reed are discussing something. Everyone becomes quiet when I sit down.

Molly looks at me. "That was so weird, Jay. We were just talking about how Coach B just blew that up. I wonder what set him off?"

Shrugging my shoulders, I take a drink of my soda. JT looks at me and then looks at Reed. They share some unspoken conversation. Something is up with them. JT turns back to me and grabs my hand.

"Molly and Reed said that you all are going out tonight. I wish I could come, but you know that we have mandatory curfews during football season, and my parents are riding my butt." His cheeks redden a little as he continues. "I'm already in trouble with my parents for going downtown to see Rhye last night. Thank goodness, they aren't going to say anything to Coach."

I look at Molly, and she is glancing between both of us. "We could just go get dinner or something if you want us to wait until after football practice?" Molly asks as she looks at me for an answer.

"I'm cool with that JT, if you want us to wait."

"We've been having late practices. I want you to go and have a good time. I'm not the only one who has waited forever to spend some time with you."

That's why I have to love JT. I know that he would love to spend time with me, but he is thinking about Molly and Reed too. I can't help myself when I lean over and kiss his cheek.

"We'll plan something for the weekend if it's okay with you?" He nods.

We continue to talk for the remaining lunch period. Molly, Reed, and I make plans to go dancing tonight. Molly and I discuss what to wear while JT and Reed talk about the upcoming football game. The whole time, I am conscious of JT. He constantly rubs my arms or hands and stops just to smile at me. It is clear that we both deserve this chance.

Holding my hand, he walks me to my Art class. When we get to the room, he stops me before I can walk in the door. He leans against the wall and pulls me toward him to whisper into my ear.

"Jay, I have been so lost without you. Don't make me go back to how things were. I don't think I could handle it."

Closing my eyes as I listen, I nod to him. I knew it. Everyone has told me this, but to hear him say it kills me. I blink back the tears and lean my head on his shoulder. Inhaling his scent, I let all of our memories swamp me.

"Did you talk to him last night? I don't know if I can handle seeing you with him. How does he feel?"

A lump develops in my throat, but I talk through it. "He told me to pick. You or him."

JT nods his head like he agrees. "What did you tell him, Jay?"

I can't tell him that I picked Kane. In this moment, standing here with JT, I can't remember why I chose Kane. It just feels so right being with JT. I realize when I'm in his arms it is everything I've missed.

"I'll talk to him, JT." He lets me leave it at that. Placing his hand underneath my chin, he tips my face up to his.

"This is where we were always supposed to be. When you're not with me, I want you to try and remember this feeling." He kisses my lips. "I will not have gym with you this week, but I'll come see you when school lets out if I can." I nod and turn to walk into the classroom.

Molly and Reed are already sitting down. Molly smiles and waves at me. We are on opposite sides of the Art room, so we all work on our projects during class. I debate if I should text Kane that we need to talk again because I have to let him go. My heart and head know this now.

"Jay, can I have a word with you after class please?" Miss Kell's voice pulls me from my thoughts.

"Yes Ma'am," I answer her. I have no clue what she wants. Finally, after what feels like forever, the bell rings for the end of class, and I reach down for my book bag. Molly tells me she'll meet me in the parking lot and everyone else clears the room. Walking towards Miss Kell's desk, I notice that she looks upset.

"You wanted to see me?"

"Yes. Thanks for staying, Jay. Listen there's something that I have wanted to speak with you about for quite some time. I don't know how to say this, so I'm just going to ask you. Is Coach Branch bothering you?"

I know immediately that she reads the panic in my eyes. She stands up and walks around the desk to me, placing her hands on both of my arms.

"Listen, closely to me. I can help you, but you have to let me. Do you want me to help you, Jay?"

I shake my head, not wanting or needing her help. Why can't everyone leave me alone? I am just now getting my life back again, including my friends and boyfriend. What else do they want from me?

"Listen to me, Jay. I see the way he looks at you, and I see the way you react to him. Everyone thinks he walks on water, but I know differently. Did something happen? Please, let me help you."

I am unable to stifle the sob that rises from me. Miss Kell hugs me as I cry on her shoulder. After a few minutes, I calm myself. Glancing up at her, I see that she also has tears in her eyes.

"I need to go." I pull myself out of her arms. She lets me go and just looks at me.

"Jay, you need to talk to someone. You need to tell. If I could do it for you, I would, but the smug bastard thinks he's untouchable because of his position within the athletic department." I shake my head and turn away from her.

Walking out the door, I don't look back. I run straight to my car, only stopping when I see the motorcycle in front of it. Kane is standing next to it, and JT is standing next to my car. They're talking to each other, but I can tell it's pretty volatile. Neither of them sees me, and I can't handle this shit right now.

"You need a ride?" I turn, and Rhye is getting into his car.

Without thinking, I get into his passenger side, and Rhye pulls out of the parking lot. The guys never notice.

"Where to, Jay? I can take you anywhere you want to go," he says to me. I turn to Rhye and stare at him.

"Wherever, you're going. I just don't want to go home right now." He drives to his friend Chris's apartment. We used to hang out here when I was seeing him. My phone vibrates, and I look at my text messages.

Kane – Are you still at school? I'm at your car. We need to talk.

JT – Jay…where are you?

I think about ignoring them, but I can't afford for them to tear down the school looking for me. Plus, I can't have JT missing anymore football, so I text them both the same message.

Me – Need some time away. I'm good…with a friend. Don't worry. Will text you later.

I turn my phone off and slip it back in my book bag. Rhye and I go upstairs, and we can hear the music blaring from the outside. Chris lets us in, and Rhye leads me to the living room and sits down on the couch.

"You want a smoke?" I hear Chris ask Rhye, and he nods his head. He lights one up and inhales deeply. Then he offers it to me. Looking at his hand, I nod my head and take a deep drag to hold it in. After a minute, I let out the smoke and pass it back to Rhye.

We sit there not talking to one another, passing it back and forth until it burns down. Finally my mind goes numb and my body feels loose. I can feel Rhye's gaze on me, and I turn towards him.

"How did you know?" He knows what I was asking, so I do not have to explain myself.

"Jay, you were "Miss It" from the time we all were in elementary school, and I mean that in a good way. You weren't only pretty, but sweet to everyone too. The girls wanted to be you, and well, the boys wanted to be in you." I playfully hit his arm at his raunchy joke. He laughs and continues, "Sorry, but it's true. Then our sophomore year, the girl who was always smiling, well she just quit. One day she's at school, and the next she is out sick for a month, but when she comes back, that girl is gone. This new girl is hurting. It was so obvious, but I think those close to you couldn't see it. They were hurt and mad that you pushed them away so easily." He turns all the way towards me and leans in.

"Then when you started showing up at our band practices, I knew you were looking for an escape. I could offer that to you with the alcohol and drugs. Then, we started sleeping together and I was just so damn proud that you chose me, but I learned fast enough that you didn't choose me. You weren't with me for me; you were with me for the escape." Pain fills his voice. I lean over and lay my head on his shoulder.

"I would ask you questions about your future, and you wouldn't answer. When you did, it was to put me off. You started to ask questions about which pills were dangerous to take with what, and then I noticed, when you bought those same combinations." He pauses and takes a deep breath and continues, "You used to talk in your sleep after you would pass out. Nothing specific, but I got the gist of what happened to you. Then that night we were together, I was going to tell you that I was in love with you, but you called out JT's name."

He ran his hand down my hair. "I've always known what you planned and prayed that you wouldn't do it. I tried to watch for signs, but I didn't know what to do. So I've spent the last year higher than normal because I didn't know how I was going to handle it when I got the call that you overdosed."

"I'm sorry I hit you for speaking the truth," I reply. "It sounded so ugly being spoken out loud. My plan was to cut myself off from everyone so that it wouldn't hurt as much. Rhye, I knew that I could hang out with you to get access to the drugs, but falling for you was not in my plan. You were really the first person that I had a choice to sleep with. It started out as my desire to have control, but then I developed feelings. I don't recall saying JT's name when I was with you, but I probably did at that time because I was messed up. I'm sorry for that, but it hurt me when you slept with that groupie too."

I sit up straight and turn towards him. "Rhye, you kind of saved me. At first, I planned on taking those pills as soon as I got them, but then you happened. All I know is that I would choose the time and place, but I chose not to at that time, because of you. I wanted to be with you. You helped me forget what happened and taught me how to enjoy sex. You showed me how to turn pain into pleasure. You did Rhye, not JT." I feel like I owe that to him, because it is the truth.

My buzz is coming down. "I'll always love you for that, but right now that's not enough for us. Trust me, you don't want into this three ring circus I've got going on. I am not over JT, and well, you met Kane the other night. It's unfair of me to ask you to be my friend, but I could really use one right now."

"Jay, I'm here for you. Whatever, you need." He leans his forehead against mine and looks into my eyes.

I smile at him. "Thanks Rhye." I yawn and can barely hold my eyes open. "I'm going to just take a nap, okay?"

"Lay down, Jay. I'll watch over you." I lay my head in his lap, close my eyes, and fall asleep.

Chapter Nine

My head is pounding like a steel drum is beating from the inside out, and my eye lids feel heavy when I try to open them. I grimace because my body is so stiff. When I finally open my eyes and move, I realize that I'm not in my room. Everything rushes back to me, and I remember going to sleep on Rhye's lap in the apartment, but I'm not there now. However, I know exactly where I am at.

JT's room hasn't changed much these last two years. I'm in his bed, but I'm alone. I slowly rise, realizing I only have on one of his t-shirts and my panties. My clothes from yesterday are laid over his desk, so I grab my jeans and pull them on.

Opening the door from his bedroom, I follow the sound of voices to his parent's kitchen. Their voices are muffled, and I can't hear what they are saying. The smell of bacon is strong, and my stomach growls. As I walk through the door, they all stop and stare at me. JT and his mother are standing at the stove while she is cooking, and Kip is sitting at the table.

I smile at all of them. "Good Morning." I've always liked his mother, but I wasn't sure how she felt about me as the result of these last two years. She smiles back and walks over to hug me.

"Hey, Jay, honey. How are you feeling this morning?" Her eyes are kind, and she looks over me. "I called your mom and dad last night to let them know that you are here. Your mom wanted you to call her once you got up."

"Thanks, Mrs. Higgins. I'll call her in a second." Does she know that I was passed out high as a kite last night? I need to talk with JT and find out how I got here. "Uh JT, can I talk to you a second?" Looking at him, I realize that he looks mad.

He nods his head and walks to the back door, opening it for me. As I pass by Kip, he whispers to me, "He's pissed. Good luck." Just great, I think to myself as I follow him into his backyard.

JT walks over and throws himself on a lounge chair then glares at me. I decide to just stand in front of him. He raises his eyebrow at me and folds his arms over his chest. He starts to speak and stops to shake his head. I wait for him to say something.

"Do you remember me coming to get you?" I shake my head. "Do you remember my mom helping you to bed?" I shake my head again, and my cheeks blush. "Damn, Jay."

"How did you know where I was?" My voice is hoarse.

"Your boy Rhye called me to come get you. He told me that you saw me and Kane at your car and panicked. He's always in the right place at the right time, isn't he? Rhye to the fucking rescue." His voice is bitter.

"Rhye called you to come get me?" I say confused.

"Yeah, he called me from your phone and told me where you were. He said that you needed me, but he left out that you were passed out cold. Lover boy said you kept calling my name in your sleep. Do you need me, Jay? Because that's not what Kane, told me yesterday. He told me that you had chosen him. That you were his."

"What happened after school?" I had to ask.

He laughs. "I went out to wait for you at your car and he was already there. He said that he wanted to talk to me. Pretty much he told me what I already know. You've had a rough couple of years and that neither one of us needs to push you right now. He went on to say that I needed to give you space and that you had chosen to be with him. We talked a little and then both of us got your text." He looks at me and his blue eyes bore into mine as he stands up.

"I want you, Jay, but I want you happy first. Damn it, if that's him then, I'll back off." His voice breaks and he swallows hard. He wraps his arms around me and pulls me close, whispering against me. "As long as I know you're in this world, I can do that. If you weren't here, Jay," he stops talking and just holds me tight.

I rub his back as his body shakes against mine. For once, my mind is clear and I now know what I want. No second guessing this time. Someone is going to be hurt, but this life is too short, and I've wasted too much of it. I pull back from JT and look into his eyes, needing to be completely honest with him.

"JT, I am so sorry, and I've made a horrible mistake." He tries to pull away from me, but I hold tight. "Listen to me for just two seconds. I did tell Kane that I would be his, but it was because he wouldn't give me time to let me decide what I wanted. After I talked with you the other day, I went back to him and asked him for time to figure things out with you, but he gave me an ultimatum, and I panicked. The next morning, when I saw you, I knew that I had made a mistake. I've been so confused. At one time, you were everything I ever wanted. I saw my future whenever I looked at you. The past two years I haven't allowed myself any real connections and then Kane came along. I do care about him, deeply, but JT it's nothing compared to how I feel about you."

I take a deep breath and softly kiss his lips. Tears roll down both of our cheeks. "If you will have me, I will promise to live for you. To give up the past and only be with you, forever. I love you, JT. Please forgive me," my voice cries, and he crushes me to him.

"This is it Jay, because I'm not ever letting you go. Do you understand me? There will not be another minute of my life without you in it. God, I love you baby. I love you so much." He kisses my lips over and over, whispering his feelings for me. I could have stood there forever, but a voice clears itself from the door. We both turn, and Mrs. Higgins is standing there, with tears in her eyes.

I didn't know what she would say or do, but she surprised us both. She walks over and envelops us in her arms. She should hate me; I would hate a girl if she put my son through half of what I put JT through. At that moment, she speaks, and it's almost like she could hear my thoughts.

"I just want both of my children to be happy, Jay, and you make him very happy. He's been miserable without you. Just love each other and everything else will fall in place." She clears her voice, and continues, "But now you two are going to be late for school. JT go ahead and get dressed. You'll need to take Jay to her house for some clothes." He smiles at me and turns to go in.

"Thank you," I smile and tell her.

"No, thank you. I don't know what happened with both of you, but I'm no dummy. Just love him, Jay. You're the one for him."

"I know now that he's the only one for me, too." We hug once more and walk back inside. Running upstairs, I grab my bag and we leave for my house.

Sitting in his truck, I realize I need to call my parents, so I reach for my phone. I have over thirty text messages and calls. Most are from Kane, JT, and Molly wanting to know where I was yesterday. One was even from Reed. A couple of them are from my parents, but the last two text messages sent from my phone, catch my eye. They were sent to Kane's phone.

Me – This is JT. She is safe. Rhye called me to come and get her because she had passed out. My mother is with her now.

Me – I'll have her call you in the morning.

Kane – Thanks

Rhye had also sent me a text this morning.

Rhye – Here for you always. I called the one for you. See you around.

JT looks at me as I read my phone.

"I sent him a text from your phone to let him know you were okay and with me." He looks at me sheepishly. "I didn't do it to hurt him or anything. I would have wanted to know you were okay if he had been the one Rhye called."

Leaning over the truck console, I kiss his cheek. "That's why I love you so much."

We arrive at my house minutes later, and Kane's silver Crossfire is parked in the driveway. JT looks over at me.

"Give me your house keys, and I will go on inside to wait for you." I nod and give them to him.

We both climb out of his truck and Kane gets out of his car. JT nods at Kane and walks by us both going up to the house. He stops at the front door and looks back at me before he unlocks it and continues inside. My eyes go to Kane's; I can tell that he hasn't slept again.

"I'm sorry." I don't know what else to say.

He nods his head and says, "So am I. It's unfortunate really. I think we could have had something special. We really didn't have a fair chance, but I need you to know something, Jay. I don't hate you. I'm hurt. I realize that I backed you into a corner the other night, and I know you meant what you said, but that didn't change your feelings for him, did it?"

This time I shake my head no. He sighs and rubs the back of his neck. Glancing up to the house, he asks, "If he wasn't here would you have chosen to live for me? Could I have been that for you?"

"Yes, you made me want my future again. The only problem is that he was my future first." A tear slides down my cheek. He steps closer to me, but he doesn't touch me. He gently leans over and kisses my cheek.

"I love you, Jay." He doesn't look at me as he walks back to his car and drives away. I stand there for a second and wipe the tears away. JT doesn't deserve to see me cry over Kane. From this point forward, I am going to prove to him that I am worth the wait.

Walking into the house, I go to find him. He is in the living room sitting on the couch. I plop down onto his lap, and he laughs as he kisses me.

"I was holding my breath not wanting to take one second with you for granted," he says to me.

"I'm all yours." I kiss him deeply back. He stands us both up and slaps my butt.

"Go get dressed before you get me in trouble. I would miss school in a heartbeat if the first game wasn't tomorrow night. I got a future to plan now," he says, and my heart melts.

Looking in his eyes, I reply, "So do I."

Taking a quick shower, I think about the bottle of pills I have hid. I don't have time to get rid of them now, but I will this weekend. Wanting to look pretty for JT, I throw on my short white sundress with strappy white sandals and blow dry my hair straight. Adding some quick lip gloss, I take one last look in the mirror and walk downstairs.

He's waiting in the foyer, and he watches me as I walk down the stairs. I can see the hunger in his eyes. He approaches me as I step off the final step.

"You're beautiful, Jay. Thank you for choosing me."

"It was never a choice. It's always been you for me." He smiles against my lips as he brings me in for a kiss.

"Let's go to school. I can't wait to let everyone know that you're mine."

He grabs my hand and pulls me out of the house to his car. I remember to call my parents on the way there and let them know I am okay. I am pretty vague answering their questions. They said they were coming home Friday night and we would talk then. That didn't sound good.

When we arrive at school, I realize we are running a little late. Walking through the parking lot, we both laugh. JT grabs me before we go in the building and kisses me. He walks me to my first class and stops just inside of the door so that the whole class can see us. He gently cradles my face with his hands and kisses me again. You can hear the whistles from the classroom.

When he pulls back, he looks at Cal, who is already sitting down and says, "Take care of my girl." Cal lets out a big laugh and calls back to him.

"Since it seems you are marking your territory, why don't you go ahead and pee on her while you're at it?" All the guys around Cal laugh at his joke.

JT just shakes his head at Cal and looks back to me. "I'll see you after class. Love you, Jay." One last kiss, and he's gone.

Cal winks at me, and I know he's happy. I laugh because I haven't been this happy in forever. The whole day goes wonderfully. Rhye smiles at me in second period, but that is it. I apologize to Molly and Reed, and they are very understanding. We make plans to hang out at the football game Friday night followed by the party afterwards at Cal's house. It was like the last two years hadn't happened, and this was how my life was supposed to be.

JT takes every chance he could to let the school know we are back together. During lunch, he makes sure he is in constant contact with me. He alternates holding my hand with rubbing my arm. In Art class, Miss Kell smiles at me, but doesn't try to talk to me again. Hopefully, she realizes that I am moving on.

After school, JT walks me to my car that had been here overnight. He has football practice, so he kisses me goodbye and says, "I'm coming straight to your house tonight after practice. I won't be able to stay long because of the football curfew, but I need to see you before I go to sleep."

"I'll be waiting for you."

While JT is at practice, Molly, Reed, and I go shopping and out to dinner. We have a great time, and before I know it, I am home waiting for JT. I bought a new red dress for the game tomorrow night. Red is his favorite color, and I know this little strapless number will drive him crazy. It is finally time for me to have JT.

I hear the doorbell ring just as my thoughts are getting good. Smiling, I open the door for JT, and he is grinning right back at me. Jumping into his arms, I wrap my legs around his waist and kiss his lips.

"Happy to see me?" He laughs at me, but I know he love this.

I bite his bottom lip and suck it into my mouth. My body trembles when he groans. I kiss deeply, and he walks inside with me wrapped around him. I kick the door closed. He carries me to the stairs and all the way up. When we make it to my bedroom, he sets me down and looks at me.

"Are you sure, Jay?"

I nod my head at him and say, "I've waited forever for you. I don't want to wait another minute."

He grabs me and kisses me deeply. We both remove our clothes within seconds. I stand back and look at his body. He has a man's body now with sinewy muscles from football. Running my hands up and down, I commit every crease and crevice to memory. His blue eyes are vibrant, and the love shines through them.

He looks into my eyes and says, "My turn." He bends my head to the side as he kisses my neck and traces his mouth down my body. "I love your body, Jay. My dreams didn't do you justice." There is a smile in his voice. He kisses both of my breasts and runs his hands down my stomach. He grabs my hips and pushes me back on the bed, but he doesn't follow. Leaning back and grabbing his jeans, he pulls out a condom..

"We'll take this slow. Tell me if I rush you." He lies down beside me and smiles. His strong hands trace up and down my body as he kisses my neck. I pull him toward me.

"JT, don't make me wait any longer." My breath is coming quicker, and I ache for him. He climbs over me making sure not to rest all of his weight down. Looking into my eyes, he grins again. He opens the condom and puts it on.

"I love you, Jay," he says as he slides into my warmth. It feels so good, and I feel so full. JT groans and says, "Forever Jay. I am going to love you forever." His movements are slow at first, with both of us enjoying the moment of finally being together.

JT's body quivers above mine, and his movements quicken. My body reacts to his and we are both breathing heavily now. "Come for me, Jay. I can't wait baby." My body explodes with his words, and he follows. He lays on top, resting his weight on me. I run my hands up and down to the middle of his back.

After a minute, he rolls off and kisses me on the lips before walking to my bathroom. My body hums with contentment. I watch him come through the door. He is gloriously naked as he slides next to me in bed. He laughs when he looks at my face.

"Your eyes are lighting up like you want more. You'll have to give me a pass on a second time. If I didn't have a football game tomorrow night, I promise you wouldn't be able to get rid of me. In fact, Jay, I've been thinking about something."

I tear my eyes away from devouring his body and answer him, "What?"

"I want to get married."

Now he has my attention. I give a nervous laugh. "Ok, maybe someday?"

"No Jay, I want to marry you now. We've wasted so much time, and life is way too short. I know we are just in high school, but I know I want to spend my life with you. It's not enough to be with you. I want to sleep next to you every night and watch over you so I can keep you safe."

"Have you lost your mind? We are just now starting our senior year of high school. Then you have college, and hopefully now, I might too. I'll marry you, but sometime way off in the future." I'm stunned.

"Maybe I have, Jay. These past two years have changed me. I'm afraid that if close my eyes, you will disappear, and that scares me. I was so afraid that I would get here tonight and you wouldn't let me in. That you had changed your mind." He snuggles me closer to him.

"I'm not going to change my mind. Not ever. No matter what happens, it's you and me." Looking into my eyes, he nods at me.

"Just think about it, okay?" I don't want to fight with him, so I nod yes. "I've got this stupid football curfew, and my mom warned me to only stay an hour. Can I stay tomorrow night?"

"My parents are supposed to be home, but we'll work something out. We can always stay at Cal's." I wiggle my eyes at him, and he starts tickling me, making me laugh out loud.

"Yeah, we can do that," he says happily as he gets out of bed. Crossing my legs, I sit on the bed and watch him dress. Before he goes into the bathroom again, he throws me a t-shirt and panties.

"Get dressed so you can walk me out."

"Yes Master," I say and laugh.

He mutters, "I wish."

Once we are both dressed, I walk him downstairs.

"Jay, I hate to leave you. It's tearing me up inside. Think about what I said. Okay?" He kisses me and groans. "Love you. Lock the door and turn on the alarm."

"Love you too." My voice shakes. All the emotions that I feel for him rush at me. He's finally mine, and tears cloud my eyes.

"Jay, what is it? You're scaring me baby." He grabs me and pulls me towards him.

"I'm just happy," I say. He kisses me and steps back.

"Me too, Jay. Me too."

"I'm okay. Just go. I can't wait to sit in the stands tomorrow and cheer you on." I raise my face to his and kiss his cheek.

"And I'm sleeping with you tomorrow night, right?" He asks me. I nod my head because too many emotions are choking me up. He kisses me one last time and walks out the door.

I go upstairs after I lock the house up. Turning some music on from the playlist on my phone, I decide to check my text messages. I had a couple.

Molly – Party tomorrow night!!! Are you and JT going to stay at Cal's? I love typing "you and JT" ☺

Jill – What happened with Kane? He got pretty hammered tonight and when I ask about you he told me to talk to you. Hope you're okay sweetie…

Mom – We'll be home late tomorrow night. Love you!!!!

I text back Molly first.

Me – We'll probably stay at Cal's. I'll talk to you tomorrow. Can't wait to hang out with you guys.

Texting Jill back is harder. I didn't know what to say.

Me – I'll talk to you later about everything. Kane and I are done. I am back with JT. Long story. I'll come see you next week.

While I am texting her back, my phone chirps.

JT – Tonight was worth the wait. You are my LIFE. Love you.

Me – Yes it was. Love you!!!

I lay down in my bed, still smelling JT on my sheets. Cradling my pillow to me, I fall asleep thinking about him.

Sitting against the bathroom door, I look at the test I hold in my hand. Two fucking pink lines. It's the fifth test I've taken in the last hour. I had driven to the next town so no one would see me buy the pregnancy test kits. They all had the same results after I had peed on them. I think back over the last month.

The first two weeks after the rape I told everyone that I had the flu. My teachers sent my homework home, and since I had never missed school since kindergarten, no one questioned me. The only problem was me refusing to see Molly, Reed and JT. They had started to get a little suspicious. My mom is there every day taking care of me and delivering the news that I didn't feel good.

The third week home I knew that I would have to go back to school. I called JT that night and told him that I needed some time apart. Shocked into silence at first, he then begged me to come over, and he did. My dad kept him away from me. Finally, after a couple of nights of him camping on the front yard and blasting love songs toward my windows, I went out and told him there was someone else. He broke down in front of me and called me a whore. Maybe I was.

Breaking things off from Molly and Reed was harder. I picked a fight with Molly when she finally got past my mom one afternoon at my house. It pretty much, "nailed the lid shut", on our friendship when I told her that she is way too immature to hang out with and that she needed to grow up. I had known for years that Reed secretly loved Molly, and I knew that me being mean to her would turn him against me.

The thought of getting pregnant never crossed my mind until yesterday morning. I became nauseated as soon as I woke up. Knowing that I am a week late on my period should have clued me in, but the combination of both got me to thinking. Leaving my house for the first time in weeks, I drove to the drug store in the next town over. I stood in the aisle and stared at the tests. Tears rolled down my face. I knew what the outcome would be. I grabbed five different tests, checked out, and drove home.

My mind races with a million thoughts. The world didn't stop for me, and it wouldn't stop if I weren't in it anymore. I pushed away those who would hurt the most. What would it take to end it all? I don't think I could pull the trigger or cut gashes into my wrist. The most logical for me would be to go to sleep and not wake up.

First, I have to take care of this. My cousin told me about a place that a friend of hers went to last year to have an abortion. I call her to get all the information, and schedule the appointment for the next day. My cousin offers to take me, so I call her back and swear her to secrecy. She picks me up the next day. I tell my mother that we are going shopping and then spending the weekend at her apartment. She's just happy that I'm getting out.

The next morning, my cousin drives me to the clinic. I sign in, and a nurse takes me back to a room. She performs an ultrasound and then directs me to her office. She explains the procedure and then asks me again if I understand. I nod to her. She has me undress and put on a white hospital gown. Afterwards, she leads me to a small white room. Metal chairs line the walls, and girls of different ages and ethnicities sit in them.

At first, no one says anything, but then one girl begins to talk about why she is here. She says this is her third abortion, and evidently, this is her choice of birth control. After she finishes, an older woman says that she has a disease that could be passed on to a child, so she is choosing to abort. One after another, they lay down their sins, maybe looking for atonement that I already know will never come.

When everyone had spoken but me, I look down at the floor and take a breath. "I was raped," I whisper into the silence. I don't look up, and no one says anything else. Eventually, a nurse comes in, and one by one calls our names. I am led to another room and placed on a table with my feet in stir-ups. The doctor talks to whoever was performing the anesthesia about where they plan to play golf that afternoon. He tells me to count down from ten. I don't remember anything past eight.

Opening my eyes, I wake from my dream. Sometimes people actually live real life nightmares, and that day for me was one, but it's over. I survived. It's still dark outside, so I close my eyes to go back to sleep.

chapter Ten

My alarm blares on the table beside me, jarring me from deep sleep. It's Friday, and I am going to cheer JT on tonight. A smile spreads across my face and I jump out of bed to shower. I dress in our school colors, a red shirt and short black skirt, because we are having a pep rally during last period today. Throwing together an overnight bag, I grab the dress to take with me for the party after the game.

Downstairs, I start to fix my coffee when the doorbell rings. Seeing JT standing at the front door in his football jersey and jeans, takes my breath away. Could he be any cuter? I open the door, and he is smiling at me.

"I really like that skirt." He says to me and grabs my hips as he pulls me towards him. "Kiss me good morning, Jay."

I lean in to him and kiss his lips. He has on the same cologne he used to wear when we dated before. The same smell that was on my sheets from last night. I try to pull him into my house, but he stops me.

"Oh no Jay, don't do this to me. We have to go to school. I am going to play my hardest at the game for you tonight and win. Afterwards, I'm going to show you off at Cal's, then I'm going to lock you up in a room somewhere and we are not coming out for a long while."

Smiling at him, I nod my head and say, "Sounds like a good plan to me." I grab my bag and dress to head out the door. I notice him checking out my outfit for tonight.

"Please say you are wearing that for me." His voice sounds so husky.

Looking innocent, I shrug my shoulders and tell him, "No, it's for Cal." He swats my behind with his hand playfully.

"I know you bought it for me because it's my favorite color, so don't lie. Plus, Cal wouldn't know what to do with you in that dress, but I do." He grins and slings my bag over his shoulder so that he can pick me up to carry me to his truck.

We reach school, and everyone is hyped up about the game. Red and black streamers cover most of the cars in the parking lot. After we park, many of the players come over with their girlfriends to talk to us. It's like JT and I have never been apart. Cal, Molly, and Reed, along with some other people, join us, and we all talk about the game and the party tonight. The only person I see standing away and not looking happy for us is Stacie, JT's ex-girlfriend. I hadn't thought about her since that day in the cafeteria.

Molly says something to me, so I turn back to her. We decide that I will catch a lift to her house to get ready for the game and then ride to the party with JT. The gathering breaks up, and everyone heads inside. JT places his arm around me proudly as we walk to class. At the door, he starts to kiss me when a voice interrupts us.

"Mr. Higgins, I need to see you in my office." Coach Branch glares at JT. It's almost like he was waiting for us. JT turns back to me and starts to say something. "Now, JT! Go on into class, James." He nods for me to move. I do as he says and walk into class.

"What happened with, JT? I could see you both talking to Coach B outside the door," Cal asks.

I shrug my shoulders and sit at the desk. Mrs. Davis starts class as soon as the bell rings. My thoughts run wild about why Coach Branch looked so angry outside the classroom. I can't figure out what he wants from me. My mind drifts, and before I know it, the bell rings. JT is waiting outside the door.

"What did he want, JT?"

"I don't know any more, Jay. Lately, all he does is ride my ass about you and threaten my scholarship chances if I don't leave you alone. I swear he acts like he's your dad or something." JT looks upset.

"Can he really take away your scholarships?"

"Hell no, I'll earn them for my athletic ability alone. There are some guys that he will be the only reason they get a full ride to college, but not me. I just don't understand what his problem is."

I swallow hard and turn away walking to my next class. He catches up to me and slides his hand into mine. Glancing down at our intertwined fingers, I watch as he lifts our joined hands and kisses them.

"It's you and me against the world, Jay. The way it always should have been." He looks at me.

Smiling at him, we arrive at my next class. Before we go in, I look up to see Rhye walking in as well. JT looks at him and actually smiles.

"Hey, Rhye." He lifts his head in greeting. Rhye nods his head back and looks at me.

"Morning, Jay." He smiles and walks by, not waiting for me to respond.

JT surprises me because I don't expect him to be so friendly with Rhye. I know I have a puzzled look on my face. He shrugs his shoulders at me.

"He called me to come get you. I would almost say, other than you right now, he's my favorite person. Believe me, I never thought I'd say that," he comments with a laugh as I walk into class shaking my head.

When lunch period finally arrives, I walk down to the cafeteria with JT. Molly and Reed are already sitting at our table when we sit down. More people join us, just like this morning in the parking lot. Most of the guys are talking about the game tonight, and the others are talking about the party.

"Did you bring that hot dress for tonight, Jay?" Molly asks.

"Yeah, it's in JT's truck. I'll get it this afternoon." My conversation must have caught JT's attention because he stops talking to one of his players and turns to me.

"Don't let me forget to get my phone out of my truck. I could have sworn, I brought in with me this morning, but it's not in my pocket."

"Ok," I say. He leans down and kisses my mouth sweetly, and everyone at the table groans. Suddenly, we are hit with a battalion of french fries.

Reed yells, "Get a room!"

JT just smiles at me and whispers, "I plan to."

After lunch, I walk with Molly and Reed to Art class; JT has to get ready for the pep rally. We are starting a new project in Art, so we opt to be in a group together. Molly asks me about last night, and I share with her. Reed just ignores us. It's nice to have her back.

Before class is over, my phone buzzes with a text message.

JT – Need to talk to you. Meet me in science lab after class during pep rally. Don't tell anyone.

He must have found his phone. I wonder why he wants to talk with me. Hearing my name, I turn around when the bell rings.

"Jay, are you coming to the pep rally with us?" Molly asks.

"I forgot to get something out of my locker. Go ahead, and I'll meet you guys there. Okay?"

Molly nods her head, and I head over to the science lab. Everyone around me is heading towards the gym for the pep rally. I walk directly to my locker to waste some time and arrange the contents. When the final bell rings and the hallways are vacant, I walk towards the science lab.

I open the door to the lab, and it closes behind me. They're several exit doors propped open leading into the room. It's not that private, but I'm guessing JT is figuring that all the students and staff will be in the gym. Walking into the room, I sit my book bag down on a work station.

Hearing footsteps, I turn around thinking I'll see JT, but it's not him. Coach Branch stands behind me with JT's phone in his hand. His face is contorted with anger.

"You stupid whore. Really Jay, you think I'm going to let him have what's mine? I don't think so." He walks toward me, and I back up.

Hysteria rises in me, but I know I can't panic right now. "What's yours?" I look at him.

"You, Jay. You might have shared yourself all over town these last two years, but at least you weren't giving it to him. I've never liked that little shit. Actually, you being a little loose has really helped me out Jay. I mean who would ever believe a drug addict whore over this school's star coach, loving husband, and father? No one Jay. No one would ever believe you." He laughs and looks down at my body.

"I've never told anyone. I never plan to." My voice shakes with tears and terror.

"Oh, I'm not talking about that. I'm talking about how I'm going to take that little body again and again. I've been missing you, Jay. You throw my notes away and ignore me. That hurts me, and it makes me angry. I'm going to have to punish you for your sins."

My head jerks up at his comment. "Punish me?" I step further away from him, but he advances on me.

"Yes Jay. Maybe you think I'm stupid, but I assure you, I've been one step ahead of you this whole time. I guessed right away why you weren't in school that month after we were together. Did you kill my baby, Jay?"

The color left my face, and I feel faint. He rushes forward and grabs me towards him. I know better than to fight him off. He enjoys it too much.

"You did, didn't you? Why you little murderer! What would your perfect boyfriend JT think about that?"

"Let me go," I say in a whisper. "I'll tell everyone. If you don't let me go, I promise that I will."

His chuckle is evil sounding. "Go ahead. I really don't think anyone would believe you. I'll just tell them how you threw yourself at me for years. I've already mentioned to my wife how you constantly flirt with me. She will share that with anyone I tell her to. Really Jay, you should have told when it happened. You didn't tell though did you? Maybe you liked it."

Something in me snaps, and I push his chest back with all my strength. Slapping his face hard, I can see the surprise. I scream in his face and push him hard again.

"You Bastard, what do you think I liked? That you raped me in a gym closet and then got me pregnant so that I had to have an abortion. That you ruined me for my boyfriend and my friends? You took it all away from me, and then you continue to harass me for years. What the fuck do you think I liked about any of that? I swear to all that's holy that if you come near me again, I will tell everyone. I don't care if anyone believes me. I will not stop talking about it until your own kids grow up."

I push him one more time away from me for good. "Do not come near me." Grabbing JT's phone out of his hand, I pick up my book bag to walk out. I'm breathing hard as I walk toward the gym. It's over with him. Please God, let it be over.

The noise from the pep rally is loud, and I can hear the cheers when they call JT to the stage. Miss Kell runs toward me as soon as I walk through the gym door. "James, where have you been? When I didn't see you or him at the pep rally, I started to panic."

"I'm okay Miss Kell."

She looks at my face and frowns. "You don't look okay."

"I am now. Trust me." I walk around her and into the gym just in time to see JT walk onto the stage.

Finding a seat on the front bleacher, I try to calm myself. JT is looking over the crowd for me. When he finally spots me, he smiles and starts talking into the microphone.

"Who wants to beat some Jaguars tonight?" Everyone goes

crazy yelling, "YES!" "For those of us who are seniors, this will be our last year playing high school football. We need to take it as far as we can, and I believe that's all the way to State!" Again everyone claps and yells.

"You know I'm going to play my heart out for you guys tonight, especially for my girl, Jay." He looks directly at me and smiles. "So let's go out there and leave it all on the field. Let's go Bulldogs!" Everyone stands up to cheer. He walks off the stage and heads directly to me. I see that Cal is getting up to speak, but I do not hear him because of JT.

"What is wrong, Jay? Your face is white as snow. I know when something is wrong, so please just tell me."

"If I tell you that everything is fine, will you please just drop it? I swear that if you'll do that, tomorrow I will tell you everything I can."

He looks at me and asks, "Everything, Jay?"

I nod back to him. "Everything I possibly can, without hurting too many people. Okay?" Nodding, he moves to sit beside me on the bleacher. "Are you not going back to sit with your team?"

He turns to me. "You're my most important teammate. We are my most important team. Forever, Jay."

I lean in and kiss him, "You're my M.V.P." He laughs and kisses me back.

When the pep rally ends, JT has to go back to get ready for the game, but first he walks me to his truck to get my things. I place his phone inside his truck without saying anything.

"After the game, I'll meet you outside the locker room. We'll ride to the party together. Okay?" He asks.

"Sounds good to me," I say as I lean up and kiss his cheek. "I'm going to Molly's house so that I can change into Cal's dress." I bat my eyes at him trying to be funny.

"You can say that you're putting on that dress for Cal, baby, but I'm going to be the only one that takes it off." I laugh at him.

"It's yours," I say to him and wink.

"I know," he says and winks back. "Wish me luck tonight." I tug him down to me and kiss him hard.

"Good luck, baby." At that, he smiles again.

Molly and I drive to her house to get ready. I don't talk about what happened today, but I know tomorrow I am going to have to tell JT something. Could I tell him, yes, I was raped, but not tell him by whom? Telling him who it was would not be a good idea for anyone.

"Do you want to stop off and get our nails done?" Molly asks.

"Sure Mols, that sounds fun."

We get our nails done and are back at her house by dinner. After eating something light, we go upstairs to shower and get ready. Pulling on my new dress, I look in the mirror and know JT will love it. The color is candy apple red, and it's short and sleeveless. I brought a light black jacket to wear over it for the game to tone it down little. I slide on a pair of black ankle boots. Curling my hair, I leave it loose around my face.

Molly wears the navy dress she bought yesterday. It looks good with her coloring. When she spies me, she stops, and her jaw drops.

"Damn Jay. You look hot. Don't let JT see you in that dress until after the game. He won't be able to throw anything." We don't laugh because we know it's true.

"Thanks! You look pretty spectacular yourself. Reed is going to have a fit."

We head downstairs and get into Molly's car to head to the game. "Can I tell you something crazy?" I look at her, and she nods her head. "JT asked me to marry him, and he meant like now."

"Are you kidding me, Jay?"

"No, I really wish I was. Part of me still thinks he's not serious, but another part knows that he is."

"What do you want?"

"I want JT to be happy. Whatever that is, that is what I want."

She smiles at me. "You will figure it out. You'll know when you're both ready."

I process her words and know they are correct. My mind just needs to slow down and work through everything that has happened these last two weeks. Tonight though, I'm just going to enjoy my friends and boyfriend.

We arrive at the football stadium just as our players run out on the field. The night is electric with the anticipation of the game. Every space in the bleachers is packed in tight with people. Molly and I find Reed in the student section, and we squeeze in.

Below us on the field, the cheerleaders try to get the crowd pumped while the football players warm up for the big game. All the coaches are getting ready on the sidelines, but when I notice Coach Branch looking up at me, I look away. My eyes meet his wife's. She holds their children on her lap and looks from me to him. In that moment, I feel sorry for her. She is the one that has to live with that monster, and thank God not me anymore. I turn away and promise to never look back.

The hair on the back of my neck stands up. Glancing around, I see Stacie, JT's ex-girlfriend, standing with a group of students staring at me. Some of the looks hold a depth of pity in their eyes, but others are hostile. Turning my back on them, I turn to Molly to see if she notices the stares, but she is talking with Reed. I double back, and they are gone.

A loud horn blows, and the game starts with the kick-off. When JT goes out on the field for the first time, he stops and turns around to look right up at me in the stands. He brings his hand to his heart, and then he points right at me. My smile goes from one side of my face to the other. Molly nudges my knee with hers and grins at me.

"That boy has always had it bad for you."

"I love him," I sigh.

The first possession we have of the ball, JT drives it all the way down the field and scores the first touchdown. We jump up, and the entire crowd screams for him. The game progresses fast from that point. During the second quarter, I look to the students sitting a couple of rows in front of us and notice that they are all looking at their phones. A couple of them glance back directly at me. One freshman girl has tears falling down her face while she stares at me. I grab Molly's arm again to see if she notices, but in that moment, JT throws a pass for another touchdown. She and I both jump up to cheer, and I forget to ask her.

At half-time, I finally have a chance to talk to Molly, but I feel almost dumb mentioning it. Everyone seems to be enjoying the game, and no one is looking at me now. I decide not to bring anything up and ruin the night. The second half starts, and before I know it, the game is over with us winning by twenty-four points. The crowd disperses with everyone taking their revelry elsewhere. I hug Molly and Reed as they head to Cal's house to get everything ready for the party.

Walking toward the locker room to meet up with JT, I can't help but think about the past two years. All the control I thought I had built was a mirage, just waiting to melt away. JT, Kane and, even Rhye made me feel again, but only one deserves my future. When I look up, he is leaning against the door waiting for me.

"Are you thinking about how many ways I'm going to kiss you tonight?" He asks with a smirk on his face.

"Yes, I do believe that is exactly what I am thinking about," I say as I throw myself into his arms and do just that.

He pulls back and looks at me. "I love you, Jay."

"I love you too." There's a nervous energy surrounding us. I know he feels it too.

"Let's go party it up." Grabbing my hand, he pulls me to his truck and opens the door.

"Slide to the middle and buckle up, Jay." Lifting my eyebrow in question he answers me. "Cal had to loan his truck out so that they could pick up the kegs. He is getting a ride with us to his house." As soon as he finishes talking, the passenger door slings open, and Cal flings his humongous self in.

Kissing my cheek, he smiles at me and says, "Hey, Jay baby."

"Hands off my girl, Cal," JT says as he glares at him, but I know he is kidding.

"She'll always be my girl too, just in a different way." Cal grins at me as I lean over and hug him. He really has been there for me when I didn't deserve anyone.

"Hey," JT says and pulls me to him, "quit giving my hugs away." I laugh and kiss his cheek.

We chat about who is coming tonight and what girl Cal is going to be chasing. When we arrive at his house it seems like all of our phones vibrate and chirp at the same time. Laughing, we all get out of the truck joking that our friends must be texting us wanting to know where we are. They must be anxious to get the party started.

"I bet everyone is waiting for us," JT says, but ignores his phone as do I.

"I'll catch you both later. I've got to make sure that everything is set up," Cal says as he grabs his phone, looks at it briefly, and walks off towards his house.

Looking over at JT, I slowly remove the jacket that is covering my dress and throw it back inside the truck. His eyes move up my body, and he takes a deep breath. He lets out a slow whistle. "Damn Jay. You're all my Christmas and Birthday presents combined." I let out a soft laugh.

"And I don't deserve you." I tell him as we kiss. He reaches for my hand, and we walk toward Cal's house.

Walking through the front door, I immediately see Molly crying, but that's not all. A hush falls over the house, and everyone is staring at me and JT. Most people can't even look me in the eyes, and then again, I see the hostile stares. These seem to come from mostly the football and baseball players and, of course, Stacie.

JT looks around and asks, "Last I checked we won, so why are you bunch of pansies looking upset?"

At that same moment, Cal comes running from the back of the house with his phone in his hand. His face is red, and tears fill his eyes. He grabs me away from JT and engulfs me in his arms.

"My God, Jay," he whispers and the tears roll down his big

cheeks. Cal's big body shakes as he is wraps his arms around me. "I am so sorry."

My first thought is that my parents have died in a plane crash, but before I can ask, JT grabs me from Cal. Losing my balance, I fall into his arms.

"What the fuck, Cal?" Panic and worry fill his eyes now.

Some drunken baseball player sneers at me and says, "Whore."

Whipping around in a rage, JT and Cal lunge for him at the same time. JT gets to him first and hits him square in the face.

"What's your problem, Scott?" JT yells at him.

"Your girl here probably just ruined several of our chances at a full-ride scholarship," Scott says looking right at me, "I don't believe it happened, even if I watched it. He wouldn't have done that."

"She's a druggie whore anyway," some unknown female voice whispers. There are over seventy of us standing in the room.

JT whips around and tries to find who said it. Suddenly, everything comes to me. Turning around, I grab the phone out of Cal's hand and look through his text messages. Sure enough, it seems he has received video messages, forwarded from at least fifty people in the last hour.

Pressing play, the grainy image of Coach Branch and I in the science lab fills the tiny screen. Someone must have been hiding in one of the doorways in the science lab, filming from their phone. The volume is at blast, when I hear his voice.

You Jay. You might have shared yourself all over town the last two years, but at least you weren't giving it to him. I've never liked that little shit. Actually, you being a little loose has really helped me out, Jay. I mean who would ever believe a drug addict whore over this school's star coach, loving husband, and father? No one, Jay. No one would ever believe you.

I've never told anyone. I never plan to.

Oh, I'm not talking about that. I'm talking about how I'm going to take that little body again and again. I've been missing you, Jay. You throw my notes away and ignore me. That hurts me, and it makes me angry. I'm already going to have to punish you for your sins.

Punish me?

Yes Jay. Maybe you think I'm stupid, but I assure you I've been one step ahead of you this whole time. I guessed right away why you weren't in school that month after we were together. Did you kill my baby, Jay? You did, didn't you? Why you little murderer. What would your perfect boyfriend JT think about that?

Let me go. I'll tell everyone. If you don't let me go, I promise that I will.

Go ahead. I really don't think anyone would believe you. I'll just tell them how you threw yourself at me for years. I've already mentioned to my wife how you constantly flirt with me. She will share that with anyone I tell her to. Really Jay, you should have told when it happened. You didn't tell though did you? Maybe you liked it.

You Bastard, what do you think I liked? That you raped me in a gym closet and then got me pregnant so that I had to have an abortion. That you ruined me for my boyfriend and my friends? You took it all away from me and then you continue to harass me for years. What the fuck do you think I liked about any of that? I swear to all that's holy that if you come near me again, I will tell everyone. I don't care if anyone believes me. I will not stop talking about it until your own kids grow up. Do not come near me.

When the video ends, JT grabs it from my hands and hurls it toward the wall, shattering the phone. He bends over grabbing his stomach, groaning as if he is in pain. My body is in shock. Everyone is looking at us. His sobbing brings me out of myself. Bending over, I wrap my arms around him.

"That bastard, I thought he cared about me. About all of us," he says catching his breath. "How, Jay? You were so sweet and innocent. How could he take that from me? How could he do that to you?"

I look up, and Molly and Reed are standing there. They both have been crying. Molly leans over and hugs me from behind. My body stiffens, and she pulls away, staring with pity in her eyes.

"It's okay, Jay. Everyone knows what he has done now, and he'll pay for it," she whispers to me.

"I never wanted anyone to know," I whisper back.

At my words, JT jumps up, and I fall to the ground. He looks right at Cal.

"Let's go. I'm going to beat the shit out of him." I grab him from behind.

"No JT, you'll make things worse. Just let it go. Please, for me, JT. Stay with me."

He finally turns around and looks at me, "I'll be back for you, Jay." He pushes me toward Molly and says to her, "Watch her."

He and Cal run out the door with me screaming, "Stop!" I turn to Reed and plead. "Please Reed, stop them. They'll get arrested, and what then? Please let's just go after them."

Suddenly, all hell breaks loose and everyone starts running outside to their cars. They are all going to follow JT and Cal to Coach Branch's house to catch ring side seats. I pull away from Molly and run outside to try and find my own ride. Reed grabs me from behind and pushes me toward his car with Molly.

"Get in," he tells us. I jump in the backseat, and he whips the car around out of Cal's driveway. Coach Branch lives about fifteen minutes on the other side of town through a busy intersection. When we reach the intersection nearing the house, we notice all the empty cars and trucks with their doors wide open. I hear Reed first.

"God no," he says as he jumps out of the car and starts to run with Molly running after him.

I sit in the back seat and stare through the windshield. Looking past the empty vehicles, I see the tangled heap of metal on the side of the road. At one time, it looks as if part of it was a dump truck and the other half used to be a shiny red pick-up. Slowly, almost as if my body is possessed, I get out of the car and walk towards the wreckage.

The sirens blare in the distance coming towards us. Everyone from the party is standing or sitting down crying. Molly runs up to me and tries to grab my hands to stop me, but I push her away. Someone else grabs me around the waist, and I kick and fight for them to leave me alone. Finally, I escape, running from them to the twisted metal. The closer I get, I can smell the strong scent of gasoline rising from the pavement.

I hear someone from the woods yell that they have found Cal. Looking deeply into the wreck, I can see the driver of the dump truck hanging upside down behind the wheel. He is not moving, and something dark pours from his neck. I can't stop myself from trying to look where JT should be in the red twisted metal. My heart flutters when I see he is not there.

Jumping up with hope, I look around the wreck to see if he is standing with anyone. By now, the Emergency Response Team has arrived, and they are trying to move everyone away. I hear Molly yelling for me, but I run to the woods where I can hear people crying for help. I throw my shoes off and race faster towards the voices.

"JT!" I scream for him.

I stop at the small clearing where everyone is standing and crying as they look away from something on the ground. Reed looks up at me, and tears stream down his face. He rushes forward and grabs me, trying to turn me away.

"Look away, Jay. You don't want to see this."

Fighting to get away from him, I glance back and see what he is talking about. JT lies on the ground. His neck is cocked at an odd angle, and his lifeless eyes stare back at me. The pain hits my chest like a freight train, and my body goes limp in Reed's arms.

"NO!" I scream over and over. "Please God, not him. It should have been me. It was supposed to be me!"

The paramedics come over and try to move us all away from him. Reed is cradling me in his arms as I continue to sob. Looking back, I see another body on the ground. More paramedics are performing CPR on him. Reed scoops me up and carries me away.

"Are they dead?" I hear Molly's voice, but I feel a million miles away. Reed's body shudders.

"JT's gone. I think they're still trying to save Cal," he sobs to her.

Hearing him say it, I feel a calm come over me. I know what happens now. This part I had planned all along. My voice is much clearer when I speak.

"Put me down Reed. I think I might be sick." I know that is a sure way to get away from him. Once I'm down, he pulls Molly into his arms and I take my chance. I slip away and run towards his car. My name is being called behind me, but I continue faster. Getting there first, I slip into the car and place it in reverse, screeching backwards and away.

I drive straight to my house, praying my parents are not home yet. For once, things go my way and I run in the house and lock the doors behind me. Rushing upstairs, I pull the bottle from my hiding place and start to run water in my bath. If the pills don't kill me, then maybe I'll drown.

Sitting down in the water, I turn the pill bottle up, directly to my mouth. I try to swallow as many pills as possible. Some fall into the water, but I continue turning it up until they're all gone. Then, I settle back against the tub. The water runs from the faucet, filling it by the minute, and times passes for me.

My heart thunders loudly in my head, slowing with every beat. I drowsily watch as the clear water crests over the rim of the white porcelain tub and flows over the side. Different colored pills float in the warm water. The red dress I have on seems to ripple beneath the water becoming one with the flow. I no longer feel the heaviness of my legs. My head leans back against the rim, and I slowly close my eyes. Peace shrouds me.

I have lived with this soul-burning pain for too long. I let it eat me from the inside out. It made me sick from with lies and deception. It was my hideous shame and, ultimately, my sin. I am tired of fighting. I am tired of hurting, but my decision is not based on these truths. I am here for a different reason.

With my eyes closed, I can picture his face with those shiny blue eyes that will haunt me forever. His smile as he kissed me flashes through my mind. For a moment, I feel whole again, but it's all over. It's too late. He is gone from my life. My sins were supposed to kill me, and not him. Too many people are hurt, and now everyone knows my secrets.

I think I feel his kisses on my cheek, but that could be the tears. My heart knows the truth. He is dead, and with that thought, I allow the darkness to consume me.

Chapter Eleven

Lying awake with my eyes closed in the hospital the next day, my mind still refuses to completely process the last twenty-four hours. Someone is speaking with my parents in a hushed voice that I never thought I would hear again. He is arguing with them, saying that he refuses to leave and that he will not leave me alone again. His voice breaks as he explains to them that he can help me.

Molly is crying in the background, and she is telling my mother that she agrees with Kane. She says that I love him and that he might be able to help. A nurse comes in and says that she needs to speak with my parents outside. As they leave, I hear Molly whispering to Kane.

From what I can gather, my parents were right behind me getting home last night. Molly and Reed also called the police when I took his car. Between them and my parents, my attempt only landed me in the psych ward after they pumped my stomach. She says to him that once I gained consciousness, I fought everyone in the emergency room, swearing to finish the job if they didn't let me die.

Molly asked him how he heard what happened. Kane tells her that Jill got a call from Kip, and she called him immediately. Molly wants to know if he knew about the video and he tells her he does. She then says something about Coach Branch being arrested last night. Her phone rings, and I hear her excuse herself.

I lay still as death. The screeching of a chair being pulled next to me rings in my head, and I wince at the sudden pain. He leans down with his mouth against my ear and whispers, "You can't wake a girl that pretends to sleep."

My eyes open directly to his. I try to speak, but my throat feels like someone has set it on fire.

"That's what happens when they have to put a tube down your throat to empty your stomach." His hoarse voice says as he grabs a glass of water on the table.

Leaning it towards me, he holds the straw to my mouth. I can only swallow a little bit. Clearing my throat, I try to speak again.

"Leave, I'm not going to be here long." He knows what I mean.

"You're not going to be in the hospital long or you're not going to be on this earth long?" I glare at him and shake my head.

Kane places the glass of water on the table. Leaning back down over my hospital bed, he grips the rails on either side and lowers his face close to mine.

"You listen to me, I'm not leaving you. Not for a second. Do you really think I will let myself lose another friend?"

"I'm not your friend," I whisper.

"You're right, Jay, you're not my friend. You are so much more to me, and these past couple of days didn't change that. So we'll get through this together or we will not get through it at all."

I shake my head at him and say, "I don't want you here."

He kisses my cheek and whispers back, "I'm not going anywhere."

Turning my face from him, I close my eyes tightly and choose my path again.

Note from the Author

Jay's story is far from finished. In real life, depression is an uphill battle that is not easily cured. It affects millions of people daily. If you or anyone you know have had thoughts of suicide, please, please get help.

www.**suicide**preventionlifeline.org/
1-800- 273-TALK (8255)

http://rapecrisis.com/
1-210-349-7273

Acknowledgments

First and foremost, I have to thank the most wonderful husband and father EVER. The only reason this household has clean clothes, dinner in our bellies, and most important clean sheets is because of this man. He even buys the good smelling detergent. Your Momma raised you right. Thank you for keeping the complaining to a minimum, when I locked myself away with my music blasting in my ear buds and kids running wild through the house. You're my best friend and I thank God every day for you being in my Biology class.

Thank you to my three precious hellions. Cannon you made me a mother. How can I ever repay that? I love you baby boy. Reese you are the reason I'll probably have gray hair in the next couple of years, but keep up your independent ways. It will make you a strong adult. Last, but not least, Madi Grace you have an adventurous spirit. I pray that you keep that and it takes you for a wild ride through life. Just please take me with you.

To Mom and Dad, thank you for growing a dreamer and allowing me to make mistakes, but always being there for me no matter what. I made it hard and impossible at times. Thank you for loving me anyway. I love you guys.

What can I say Lynn. You've been here since the beginning. You are like my other mother and the first person, I call for advice. Thank you for loving me and supporting me. I haven't forgotten about you Monk. You know I love you too!!!

Donna, thank you for taking the time to help me edit my book. You are one fabulous friend and your input was invaluable. Keep being the wonderful WOMAN that you are!!!

Christan...love ya girl!!! Thanks for reading chapter by chapter for me and for helping me keep Kane "douche" free...lol

To my VB club girls, Erin, Courtney, Shan, Ela, and Trina. Ya'll ladies are crazy, but I LOVE IT!!! Thank you for giving me some comic relief when I thought I was going to lose it during writing this book. Erin, you are my sister from another mister. Thanks for responding to my ten million whiney text messages. Bring on the smutty VB pics!!! We got a trip to plan Ladies!!!

ABOUT THE AUTHOR

Daughter to a pair of dreamers, you can find me thinking about what to conquer next. Life is too short, too magical, and too precious not to live full-throttle at all times!! Live yours like there is no tomorrow.

www.nicolreed.wordpress.com

Or

www.facebook.com/ruiningme